Our Time

Our Time

Gerald N. Dougherty

Pentland Press, Inc.
www.pentlandpressusa.com

PUBLISHED BY PENTLAND PRESS, INC.
5122 Bur Oak Circle, Raleigh, NC 27612
United States of America
919-782-0281

ISBN: 1-57197-318-4
Library of Congress Control Number: 2002101610

Printed in the United States of America

To Sadie and Donald Dougherty, whom God blessed me with as parents, and to my brothers Don and Fran and my sisters Ann and Mary Catherine, whom I love dearly and to my nephews and nieces, in particular Donnie, Pat and Nicky who were taken from us at too early an age.

Acknowledgments

I must acknowledge my childhood friends; Ray "General" McDonald, Joe O'Hara, Joe Collins, John "Spike" Nallen, Tom "Tucker" Lyons and his brothers Joe, Bobby and Chucky, Richard Callahan, Tom McHale, Bill and Joe Corbett, the Gallagher brothers, the Finnans and all the others who contributed to a time of innocent fun, adventure and endless summer and winter play. To my friends' families who accepted us as members of their families. To the town of Avoca, Pennsylvania, which provided us such a warm and caring environment, a town, like so many small towns across our nation, where people cared for their friends and neighbors.

I also wish to acknowledge my fellow teachers at York Catholic High School, who I'm sure were glad when the book was finished and no longer had to hear me read endless passages from it. I am most appreciative of Sister Pat Marnien, Terri Eline, Peg Allton, and Myke Warner, who patiently helped me with grammar and spelling, and also acted as my sounding board: I love you guys. To my former students who read the manuscript and encouraged me to get it published.

I'd like to thank both Ann and Emily Rockwell who typed the book for me. Special thanks and a big hug to Polly Baldwin who was gracious enough to put the book on computer disc after my original disc was accidentally deleted.

Finally, to my brothers Don and Fran and my sisters Ann and Mary Catherine who encouraged me to pursue my dream of publishing this novel.

It seems like only yesterday, that cold, gray day in early January so many years ago. Today is so much different than it was then and not just because it's a warm, bright day in June.

It took me almost half an hour to find the grave. Donald M. Docerty. Nothing else. No dates, no epitaph, nothing to indicate who he was or how he got there.

Thursday night was the last time I saw him alive. I can see him sitting there in that old gray easy chair wearing his heavy sheepskin flight jacket and that old beat up hat. He never went anywhere except to Mass without that hat. His nightly jaunt uptown to Lenny Leed's for his frosted mug of buttermilk and conversation was interrupted when he passed through the living room. I wish I could remember the program that was on television that night. It must have been good because he paused to look and stayed for the duration.

"Hey, Pop, why don't you take off your hat and stay awhile?" He ignored my stab at humor. Now it comes flooding back into my mind.

1

Friday afternoon. "Jeri, your dad was hurt very badly in the mines." Running into the house, Mom in the parlor, crying. I know without being told. My knees buckle, dropping me to the floor. My world begins to collapse.

The days and nights that followed were a blur, but not that cold January morning, not the cemetery. I'm surrounded by people but alone. Staring up at the hill as I'm doing now, a little shudder of cold comes over me and brings me back to the warm June afternoon.

Turning away from the grave I look toward the town. Pleasant Dale, Pennsylvania. It is so much smaller than I remembered. The coal hills, culm dumps and those scrawny little white birch trees that grow there. The Erie-Lackawanna Railroad yards loom in the distance. Boy, have they seen better days. The same dirt road, the old wooden bridge that leads to the cemetery have not changed since long before I was born.

How can I forget? I don't. I remember. The cold shudder I felt moments ago is replaced by a warm glow. The glow does not come from the early June sun, but from the pleasant memories of the past.

⌛

When I was a child, Pleasant Dale seemed like such a large town. The town was made up mostly of Irish, Polish and Slavic people of Catholic backgrounds. Catholic families back then were blessed with an abundance of children. We were never at a loss for kids to play with. We shared, if you can call it sharing, more than just religion. We shared a lack of material possessions, but we were rich in so many ways.

Collectively we were imaginative kids. Creativity and the ability to improvise allowed us to play without bounds. Play is the optimal word. In summer we played, ate, slept and played again. Fall, winter and spring, only school interrupted our play schedule. So our number one priority was to play. Play hard and as often as possible.

Oftentimes I hear a younger person put down someone a little longer in the tooth by saying, "That was before my time." Well that was my time, our time, the kids who formed the fabric of my life. Those were the guys who would fight with me, but more importantly fight for me. We shared that time, our time.

Standing by my father's and mother's graves, bridging a sea of time and memories, the past seems to bubble up from deep inside me like warm soda from a shaken bottle. I look out across those flat coal ponds where the water from coal wash left a black sand-like powder surface that was black as night, but oh so much fun to play tackle football on. I recall an age-old battle. Mom: "How did you get so filthy? I just washed those clothes. Well?" The perfect answer, a boy's answer: "I don't know." Of course it wasn't a lie because after all a boy really doesn't know how he gets that dirty.

Turning back to the gravesite the sadness returns. Mom's grave isn't even marked. Mom died just two years after Pop. In those two years I grew quickly into manhood. I became a sixteen-year-old man. Of course, I had to learn a lot, take things more seriously, be the man of the house. We've got to get a grave marker for Mom. We were all so young at the time, with no money. Time just slipped past.

My brothers and sisters spread out all over. My brothers, Don to Alabama, Fran to New York; my sisters, Mary Kay and Anne, down around Philly. I struggled to stay in col-

3

lege. Gone from Pleasant Dale, I never knew till now that she had no headstone. I've got to shake this feeling. Mom and Pop would be proud of us. We got what they valued: an education.

I've got to take a walk. If I remember correctly, just beyond the cemetery is a sandpit. Man, do I remember that place. We would run up the side of the bank, shut our eyes and jump, run back up the side of the bank again and jump, over and over till the sand stuck to our skin like glue, very abrasive glue I might add. Sand became a part of us, our scalps, our butts, our "unmentionable" area, down our backs, in our pockets, sneakers, inside our socks, between our toes. God it was fun.

That's where I'm going. I hope it's still there. Go ahead, Jeri. If it is there, take the plunge, one more time for old time's sake. No, let's just see if it's there. It would be a good idea if I stop talking to myself, if anyone sees me. Oh, hell with it! They probably wouldn't remember me anyway.

I'm glad I'm wearing shorts, because if I were wearing long pants all these pickers would probably be stuck to them and not my legs. I'm positive that machismo doesn't run in the family. It must just be an individual thing. I know darn well my brothers and sisters don't enjoy inflicting pain on themselves. I always hated shorts as a kid. Only sissies wore shorts, it wasn't manly. Sweating your little ass off, huh, Jeri? So Jeri, why are you wearing shorts and talking to yourself? These bushes are not nearly as tall as I remember. Then again, I was a lot shorter back then.

There it is over there. If I get a running start—Yeah right, I'll probably trip over something and then have a tough time explaining how I came to break both my arms.

I best just walk. It really has not changed a whole lot since the last time I saw it.

⧗

It was a cold, cold day in December right before Christmas. My best buddy Jim McAndrews and I were walking on the bank with our BB guns, looking for God knows what. That's when the urge hit me. I've always been struck by these unusual urges. A running start, a flying leap, rifle in hand, a soldier, a hero about to make history, save my platoon and my best buddy. Perfect leap, airborne, "Geronimo!"

I have to stop here for a second. You see, I'm older and wiser now. I learned a valuable lesson from that vault into space. The old adage should be "think before you leap" not "look before you leap." Here's a fact to consider. If the temperature stays below 32 degrees Fahrenheit for an extended period of time, things, including sand, freeze. Ah yes, the cold air rushing past, body turning in air, a nice hip to back landing. Perfect. Never better. Then reality came bouncing up to meet me. I must have bounced four feet in the air. God, did it hurt. Jim, being my best friend, didn't laugh; he just shook his head and trotted down the bank to render aid. By the time he reached me I had stopped my imitation of a slinky toy and come to rest. Just thinking of it now makes my right butt cheek hurt. As I recall, the next few days in school were spent listing to the left in my desk. You really couldn't call it a bruise. It was as if someone had spray-painted me a brilliant combination of blue, brown and black from my right shoulder all the way to my right ankle. Of course, Mom never saw or knew of it. If she had, once she recovered, she would have done to my left what I did to the right. Geez, I haven't thought of that in years. I don't mean the thoughts of the sandpit. I mean the memory of Jim.

Jim and I were best friends for as long as I can remember. His father and my father were good friends. We grew up together. I can't remember a time in our young lives when we weren't out performing deeds of heroic proportions, saving the world, fighting wars, scoring winning touchdowns.

Memories of that terrible Friday afternoon fill my thoughts once again. The house closing in on me, my legs barely able to hold me up. Got to get out—the back porch, air, away from what seemed so unreal to me at the time. There on the back porch waiting was Jim McAndrews, Joe Grady and Sean Doyle, heads down, not saying anything, just there. Words weren't necessary; actions, however, were. I can still see them standing there. I'll remember that moment till the day I die. The early teens are a time of tremendous emotions looking for ways to express themselves. At that age words always come out wrong. No words were spoken that afternoon; none were needed.

⧗

It amazes me how days seem to plod on ever so slowly while the years drop as quickly as leaves falling from trees in late October. I should drive into town and see if I can find their names in the phone book. I know Joe Grady isn't there anymore. Last I heard he was an air traffic controller in North Carolina. Good old Joe, that kid did some of the wackiest things at the time. Sean Doyle and Jim might still be around. I'm tempted to see if I can find them. I think, however, Thomas Wolfe put it aptly, "You can't go home again." We've all grown up. What would I say? Do you agree that some memories are like peaches that sweeten and soften with time? Best enjoy them as you would ripe peaches.

Since I'm dressed for the occasion, I might as well see if I can find my way back to the railroad tracks. I could go back to the cemetery, get on the tracks there and follow them. Not a good idea, Jeri. That would take you to the wrong side of town and you don't want to end up on the wrong side of town now, do you? Yuk-yuk, you made a joke. I've got to stop talking to myself. Bad sign. Sit down and think this one out.

Let's see, go back to the van, hop in and go back to Spry, Pennsylvania, or go back to the van, hop in and drive into Pleasant Dale, or get off my butt and see if I can find my way back to the old stomping grounds. Yeah, right, my un-erring sense of direction. Picture this one, Jeri. Search and rescue out of Scranton leading me out of the hills around Drury. "Ya see, fellas, I used to live around here and I thought—Why you guys looking at me like that? Ain't you ever seen an idiot before?" I'll have to use the word "ain't," you see, because it's part of the lingo of the region. "Hain't" is, of course, the past tense of "ain't."

Focus Jeri. Your mind is wandering. I think it probably would be fun just to see how much things have changed. Follow this path over toward the railroad yards. That will take me along the edge of the Creole plant then out to the road to Drury. Hang a right on the road to the tracks and it's flashback time. Ah, yes, return with me now to those thrilling days of yesteryear. Hi Ho, Jeri-o! All's I need is a little Lone Ranger theme music and away I go, broom handle between my legs and the clippity-clop noises we used to make with our mouths. There he goes folks, an idiot in action.

It's a good thing people can't read one another's thoughts because if someone were scoping in on mine now, my future would include long periods in a rubber room laced up in a neat off-white jacket with long sleeves.

Hard walking in this stuff. I'm going to be filthy when I finish this trek. Man, the railroad yards are a mess. This place used to be really busy. Coal cars loaded and going to wherever they went. Most of the stuff has been dismantled, railroad ties rotted out, old cars rusting, waiting to dissolve back to where they came from, back to the soil. Those little birch trees really cover some of the starkness of the coal dumps they're growing on. We used to peel the little strips of birch bark off, get to the sweet tasting inner bark and let it dissolve in our mouths. Christ, it's a wonder we didn't poison ourselves. I used to love to get a bottle of white birch beer soda. How could something that was clear like water taste so bubbly and sweet? I'd chug it on a hot summer day and wait for the deep belch that was sure to follow. Belching was an art form back then.

I never quite mastered the non-assisted belch, the one produced by swallowing large amounts of air in gulps, then releasing it from deep in the recesses of your stomach. I can hear it now, Joe Grady's famous twenty-five second nonstop belch. It started as a low rumble and built to a loud explosive climax, followed by applause and cheering. An art form, that try as I might, I never seemed to master. I never discovered the secret, nor would Joe ever share it with any-one. The only thing I ever got when I swallowed air was dizzy and sick. My belch would end up a barf. After barfing a few times I realized that some are blessed with talent while others are not.

Spitting was another truly prized talent. I'm not talking the phlegm-for-distance-and-disgust spit; I'm talking the between-the-front-two-teeth-for-accuracy spit. I have yet to see anyone who could equal Jim McAndrews' fine spray for-accuracy spit. He attained legendary status. I swear he could bring down a mosquito at ten feet—one shot, truly great eye-mouth coordination.

Whistling. The fingers-in-the-mouth, "come here, dog" kind of whistling, I couldn't do that either. Sean Doyle could, as could Jim and Joe, but not me. I did however gain respect and admiration from my side-of-the-mouth, high-pitched, dog barking kind of whistle. Try as they might, none of my peers could ever copy my style or reach that pitch that adults and dogs found so irritating.

One very hot August day, when Sean and I lay on our backs checking out the clouds, Sean made a discovery. A sudden flash of intuitive knowledge came across his face. He let loose with a fine spray of spit which then drifted back onto him thus cooling his flushed face. I tried but mine went up and came down the same way, as a disgusting drop. I tried again; the results were the same. Well, at least I could whistle out of the side of my mouth.

Then there was farting. What boy, given the chance to gross out his friends, wouldn't take it? We all possessed this talent. Mothers, sisters and girls found it so revolting. How many times we'd heard these words as a kid: "You hog" or "You pig." When I think of it, some farts were truly works of art while others kind of snuck up on you necessitating a return home for a clean pair of underpants, because God forbid you should ever get in an accident and die in the emergency room with soiled underwear on. What would people think?

I never realized girls farted. Of course, my sisters farted but they were my sisters. One May afternoon, Joanie Rusnizc, a fellow third-grader, and myself were picking blue bells for the Blessed Virgin Mary's shrine. Joanie bent over to pick a few flowers. As she did, she cut one. Flowers wilted in my tiny little hand. It's not possible—girls don't pass gas. They're much too delicate and genteel for such mundane things. After all they are "sugar and spice and everything nice." One expects these fragrant pauses from boys. "Darn, she probably even goes to the bathroom like guys do." So at the ripe old age of eight, a myth, held by so many of us guys fell by the wayside. When I told Jim, Joe and Sean of the episode, Jim and Joe were mildly surprised. They said their sisters farted. But Sean, he was devastated. You see, Sean had no sisters.

I wonder why just walking past the Erie-Lackawanna Railroad yards would trigger such earthy thoughts. I guess we were earthy kids. If we weren't covered in it we were rolling in it. Let's take a stroll over to the yards. Yeah, Jeri, let's.

⧖

These yards and the railroad tracks were one of our big taboos. "Stay away from those railroad cars." Every mother's nightmare was a son mangled under the wheels of a rolling train, mashed beyond recognition. The standard warning from moms, not just mine, was, "If I catch you near those trains, I'll beat you within an inch of your life." Now logically speaking, if you survived the yards without dire injury or death, Mom would end up nearly killing you. Think about it. Tell a boy never to go near something and the first thing that pops into his mind is, "Why?" He would determine that there must be something good there. It was a challenge to do it and not get caught.

Adults always want to limit good things. For instance, they are always harping on stuff like, "Eat your vegetables." Give me a break. I hate canned corn, always have, always will. "Don't go swimming after you eat." Why, will you sink from the extra weight of the food? "Don't run across the street." Wouldn't walking across increase the chances of getting hit? "Slow down, chew your food. Don't gulp it." Hey, don't I have better things to do than just sit around chewing food?

Looking around this place, I can see why they were so afraid. Just playing around the tracks was bad enough. This place is a nightmare. We did stay away most of the time and when we did get too close the railroad men would chase us away yelling statements that questioned our parents' marital status and accused us of being the little offspring of female dogs. Of course, they were right, although not about our lineage. The stories of mangled and dead kids were very real. The guy who drove the dump truck for the town of Pleasant Dale lost his arm as a kid hopping freights. Many a kid in the area misjudged the speed of an approaching train but that was them and not us. We were, after all, invincible. Bad things always happen to someone else.

Geez, this place is depressing. The railroads have long since seen their heyday and the mines are a thing of the past. Now, mostly machines do whatever mining is done.

Anthracite coal, that shiny black substance, the lifeblood of the region, at one time the major source for heating homes, was replaced by oil, gas and electricity. I threw it, shined it and shoveled it for all my young life.

It was a hard life for those who ventured into the bowels of the earth. Like a medieval king the mines both protected and destroyed those who served it. Almost without exception the mines affected my friends' families and mine. True, when I was growing up it was a dying regional resource, so in effect the region was dying economically. The glory days of mining in Scranton, Wilkes-Barre, Hazleton and Shamokin were passing rapidly and the area's second greatest resource, its people, were disappearing as quickly as the coal trucks that delivered the coal. Those immigrants and sons and daughters of immigrants were kind, hardworking and religious but hard as nails. They were forced out by the economic realities of the region.

I wonder where I would be now if Mom and Pop had moved as my aunt and uncles did? We stayed. Pop worked the mines and we grew up surrounded and protected by people like us. Just looking around I can see how physically damaged this place is. There were no environmental laws back then. The mining companies raped the land and the scars of the rape are all too visible.

I never saw those scars as a kid. To me and mine it was an ideal place to live out childhood fantasies. The breakers became old castles. Breakers were large buildings that separated slate from coal, crushed the coal into sizes, washed it and then loaded it onto railroad cars and trucks. The coal dumps were mountains to be climbed; the coal flats became glory fields where football and baseball games lasted hours until our tired little bodies dropped from exhaustion. Like a giant light show, the burning coal piles of the area mes-merized those who parked in front of them at night. The hot blue flames encased in orange-colored skin gave off sulfur-smelling fumes, but the real essence of the area more than offset the desolate looking landscape.

I better push on. Nothing left here in the yards anyway. What was will never be again. Time marches on. Thinking of my home in York County, Pennsylvania and other places like York, I notice the reverse seems to happen. There they take beautiful farmland, pave it and put in a shopping mall. They should take a place like this, pave it and put in a mall. Oh well, my answer to a lot of perplexing questions.

⧗

I've got to find that road. The road to Drury also leads to Pleasant Dale. If I can't find it, I'll have to backtrack to the cemetery. The bridge over the Demsey is on that road. The mighty Demsey Creek, tributary to the Susquehanna River. The Demsey. Its waters glistened like the colors of the rainbow with a few extras like brown and black thrown in for good measure. The only life we ever saw in or near it were rats and mosquitoes. Great combination of fauna for the area.

Many an hour was spent shooting BB gun pellets at bottles floating downstream between its not so mighty banks. We preferred to call these fights naval battles. Fleets of make-believe carriers, destroyers and even submarines were sunk in the fierce struggles. Getting the bottles was no problem. One of the two town dumps supplied us with ample amounts of Four Roses, Seagrams and a wide variety of other brand name whiskey bottles. Soda and beer bottles were never used. These, when found, were returned for cash deposits. Rounding out the fleet was a wide variety of other "use and lose" glass containers. Cans were only used when someone could smuggle a .22 caliber rifle out of the house or around the Fourth of July when firecrackers and cherry bombs were added to our arsenals. The battle plan was simple and very flexible. The warring parties occupied opposite sides of the Demsey. Bottles were launched as far upstream as we could get. We then retreated to our positions and waited. The firing commenced when the first of the glass men-o-war were spotted. It ended when all "ships" were sent to Davy Jones' locker.

One thing that was avoided like the plague was falling into those prismatic waters, waters as powerful as those of Lourdes but in reverse. Peter Paluki, a kid who lived down near the bottom of the hill that led into Drury, was gifted with physical strength that was not, however, matched by his intellectual prowess. Peter won a two-dollar bet, a sizable sum at the time. The bet was he wouldn't jump into the Demsey. The boys who raised the money were older kids from down in the area. I knew Peter, but I had only a passing "hey" kind of knowledge. Well, Peter dove headfirst into the fragrant waters. This was witnessed by one of our own crew of kids, Tommy Breslin. Tommy was better known by the nickname Tucker. Tucker was not known to fib about such serious events, so I believed him. It seems that during the two weeks following the plunge, Peter started to break out with pus-like sores all over his body. Little patches of his hair started to fall out, too. Numerous others of our gang who had seen him in the following month attested to this. I, however, never actually saw him in this condition. News of this was enough to keep us from attempting to ford those mighty waters. Only in the coldest of winters, when the stream froze, would we venture over it. There were other ways to get across, but as I recall now, they all involved some kind of broad jump and our sneakers usually got wet. This is not an option left open to me now, for jumping involves accelerated motion and I'm really only into one mode of motion at this stage and that's walking.

⧗

The road should be over that little rise. There it is. You get an A for your path finding skill, Jeri. The place hasn't changed all that much. Actually, it was easier to find than I thought it would be, I mean after all, you don't usually lose a road now, do you? Stranger things have happened in this region, however.

One day, years ago, a guy in West Scranton went down into his cellar only to find that over the course of the night the forces of nature built a sub-basement for him. Homes and buildings usually undergo a process known as settling. The weight of the building compacts the earth below it thus causing a certain amount of shifting to take place. Well, the coal regions give new meaning to the word settling. The explanation for such "unusual" settling is the random, and I use that term loosely, tunneling methods of the mine companies of the region. To put it more succinctly, they didn't know where they were going and I imagine they didn't care.

One real tragedy that occurred because of this method took place on a January day when a company tunnel under the Susquehanna River came within three feet of the bottom of the river. The roof of the tunnel collapsed causing the river to flood the mines in the area. It took two weeks to stop the flow of river water into the mines. I mean that's a whole hell of a lot of water. Of course another contributing factor to "settling" in the area was the shoring used. Wood. Now think about that for a few seconds. Mines are wet; wood rots in wet environments, ergo . . .

There I go with ergo. Jesuits really trained me well. I had a hard time passing Latin in high school but I can throw around a lot of "noto benes" and "ergos" now.

The road has not changed all that much. Like a lot of roads in Pennsylvania this one has fallen into disrepair, but I've been on worse ones around York. Probably the road to Drury was maintained better because of the bubble gum factory they built up in Drury. The bridge is up the road a piece, up past those three houses. Houses in the area were of an old-fashioned kind of structure. Built like boxes, they usually were two to three stories high. Most had dirt basements that were eventually reinforced with concrete. Ours was such a house.

It was a duplex and Pop decided to put a concrete floor on our side of the basement. He laid out the forms and planned to have the concrete poured through an open basement window. No problem, the boys would help smooth it out. Pop planned to get home around 4:00 P.M. and have plenty of time to get ready for the 5:00 P.M. delivery of concrete but the delivery actually arrived at 3:00 P.M. The fast setting concrete formed a rather nice miniature version of Mt. Fiji minus the snow. Pop arrived early, 3:45 P.M. Then the feces hit the blades so to speak. My brothers and father worked like demons to even out the ever-thickening miniature alp. I was warned not to interfere, even though I was more than willing to help, so I had to take my little play

16

shovel upstairs and keep away from the hectic scene. I never heard my Dad curse, not even once, but I suspect that day Pop was thinking, but not uttering, quite a liturgy.

Speaking of basements, Jeri, remember when Jim McAndrews and you were playing in his cellar one Easter vacation? His cellar was a lot of fun. It still had the original dirt floor and walls. Coming from mining stock we were busying ourselves trying to tunnel over to St. Marie's Grade School directly across the street from Jim's house. We were making excellent progress when all of a sudden Jim's father appeared on the stairs exclaiming, "Jesus, Mary and Joseph. What are you boys doing?" Now when those three words were used outside the confines of church or school you knew something was amiss. It seems we had almost reached a critical location underneath the foundation. Jim's father issued an edict that day, an edict that was obeyed until we reached high school age. We, Jim and I, were never permitted in the basement together—ever again, or at least I think the words were "until hell freezes over" which both of us knew would be way after the second coming of the Redeemer.

Cellars were fun, maybe too much fun because Mom was constantly yelling down the stairs at us, "What are you boys doing down there?" The standard reply was always: "Nothing, Ma." "Well get outside and do nothing." "OK, Ma." She probably thought we were doing something stupid, you know, like seeing how many clicks you could stand while holding on to the wires of a Lionel train transformer.

Another important feature of the houses in the area was the front and sometimes back porches. The porch was the center of social activity for both children and adults. I can still hear my father say, "If I had a million bucks, I'd just sit here and watch the world go by." The front porch was a place where the adults could sit and watch people on their way to or coming from church. Greetings were exchanged, neighbors came to visit, sometimes talking well into the warm summer evenings.

Of course for the kids the front porch was a shelter from the summer storms. Many a game of War was waged on those rainy days. War, the card game played with two decks of cards, was won or lost on the number of cards accumulated by the end of the game. Fish was also a card game favorite. I remember those two words, spoken so smugly, "Go fish."

Monopoly was another popular pastime, especially if it was an all day, go nowhere, praying to the Infant of Prague rain day. The prayer was a simple one, but it worked only if the tiny infant's statue was placed on the railing of the front porch near the door. Over and over, silently and aloud, the refrain was murmured: "Rain, rain, go away, come again some other day." Real panic occurred when the statue was misplaced. Frantically we would search the house, foot by foot looking for that beloved tiny little pewter figure. We had a powerful ally in our search: good old St. Anthony, patron saint of lost items. No silent muttering now, this was serious and called for verbalization: "Dear St. Anthony, please come around, something is lost and cannot be found." Over and over each passing minute increased the chances of a Noah-type rain, sure to put an end to summer vacation.

Of course, if you had a porch, you also had a crawlspace underneath the porch. Ah, what a place. It was dark, forbidding and sometimes insect-ridden. The insect most feared, the black widow, could be hiding anywhere. That added danger. What a lure. It was a place where, if we lay in wait long enough, we could scare the living crap out of somebody. We just waited until someone happened to walk by and then we screamed. This sport worked particularly well with the girls in the neighborhood.

Another alluring place was the attic. Attics were not floor covered, just beams running the entire length of the house. Attics were an ideal place to store relics from generations long past. The standard warning from both Mom and Pop was, "Stay out of there. You could fall through the ceiling." Another challenge gladly accepted. Attics were insulated; this was a big drawback mainly because those little pink fibers would get stuck all over my sweaty little body causing a severe case of itching, which was a dead giveaway. "Jeri, were you up in the attic? How many times do I have to tell you to stay out of there? Do you want to fall through the ceiling? Wait till your father gets home." That "wait till" phrase always got my attention. She never let me answer; she knew and I knew she knew so there was no point in answering. Pop would reinforce the warning when he got home. Sometimes with a slight smile on his face, for I guess he knew the lure.

⌛

So much for houses, Jeri. Not really all that many on the road up to the railroad tracks anyway. We never ventured too far down this road, at least not this far. There was not a whole lot for us to do around here. Besides it was a little too close to other kids' territory and staying away meant we remained on good terms with those kids. Those kids were a little wilder and more reckless than we, which meant we might not make it to adolescence.

Living around York for many years, I've seen growth. People move in, houses are built, and land is at a premium. Not so along this road. The land has to be cheap to draw people to it. No pristine scenes of meadows or rolling hills. The only grass that probably would do well would be Astroturf. It would look strange in winter, but no stranger than the snow we used to get around here. For years, I was under the impression that snow naturally turned black after three days, a great tourist attraction like the black sandy beaches of Hawaii.

Over the hill should be the railroad tracks. It was at those tracks our use of the road ended. The long stretch of road from Main Street in Pleasant Dale to those tracks was a straight shot. It was on that stretch that, legs pumping furiously and lungs heaving, we would attain maximum velocity on our trusty bikes. Pedal as hard and as fast as we could for the first half mile of the run then hunching over, eyes stinging from the air rushing into our crimson faces, we would soar as if we were earthbound eagles. Three, four abreast. A race to the tracks. Young hearts beating rapidly from the exertion but more from the sheer joy of life, excitement and danger. Danger was present and we knew it all too well. Thoughts of "that day" would flash across our minds. The day Joe Morin wiped out.

I remember it well. Joe, Billy, who was Joe's older brother, and I had reached terminal velocity. Joe, in the lead and intent on winning, gave that one extra pump of the pedal. That fateful pump cost Joe a lot of extra flesh that day, I'll tell you. On the downstroke Joe's pant leg got caught in the chain. That action precipitated the reaction, the sudden locking of the bike's forward motion. I didn't think he would stop sliding until he got to the railroad tracks at least a hundred yards away. We flew past his sliding body barely avoiding him. What a bloody mess. We got back to him as soon as we could. He was screaming, partially from the pain, partially from the fear. Those scars would become battle wounds, the Purple Hearts of childhood, worn proudly for all to see. The pain would fade quickly as it does with the young, but the memory would remain. Joe lost his edge that day. His own mortality caught up with him. A valuable lesson taught through experience. Like all young things, we needed to learn from these painful lessons if we were to survive and grow.

I know now that winning those races wasn't as important as being part of them.

Bicycles were the cars of the young. No gas, no pollution, no car inspections. The only fuel you needed was food. We planned no expensive repairs, only the ones we could afford.

Our family had two bicycles. One was a small, chain driven, solid rubber wheeler that had no coaster or brake. We pedaled. If we wanted to coast, we took our feet of the pedals. Braking was a real problem. Backpedaling usually resulted in injury to our legs. The only other way to stop was spragging, which was putting your heels, toes pointed up, on the ground and hoping for the best.

The other bike was one that my oldest brother Fran worked long hours to buy. It was a Columbia, a wide-tired, one speed beauty or at least it was when Fran had it. My brother Don inherited it and then passed it on to me. By the time I got it the beautiful bike was devoid of fenders, chain guard and handle grips. Its inner tubes had at least ten patches per tire. The pedals were missing two rubber pads, which gave the pedals a broad look. The pedals were now straight metal posts. Of course, it was a boy's bike. The difference between a boy's and girl's bike was the metal bar that connected the seat and the handlebars. A boy's bike had it; a girl's bike did not. This, of course, was an invention of the Marquis de Sade. Any male who ever rode a bike lived in constant fear of foot or chain slipping, causing him to come in sudden, violent contact with that metal bar. Such an event would be a day to remember, a day when he could join the Vienna Boys Choir.

My brother Don taught me to ride a two-wheeler. I was so gullible back then. I was not yet big enough to reach the pedals from the seat so I stayed perched on the cross bar. Don grabbed the seat and ran in back reassuring me that he, in fact, held the bike up. I noticed his voice was getting weaker and weaker. I glanced back. Panic. He wasn't there. I was riding on my own; he had lied. Turning quickly, or I should say just in time, I slammed headlong into a tree in front of St. Marie's Convent. The tree had heavy metal fencing around it. Boy, did that make an impression on me, especially on my face. You could have played tic-tac-toe on it. Now Don was a firm believer in the axiom, "If the horse throws you, get back up on it." So a stunned, dazed Jeri once again was in the saddle of his bucking bronco riding down Blackthorne Street followed by his older brother. Pain didn't set in until later that evening, but set in it did, the major throbbing point being my nose. This was to be one of many encounters my proboscis would have with hard, unyielding objects. All totaled, my beak was broken four times, a fact that was to plague my sainted mother through-out my early life.

Bikes provided us with ample opportunity to be creative. Baseball cards, pieces of cardboard or balloons placed so that the spokes that struck them as the wheels turned gave the impression of a motorized vehicle. We decorated, adorned, painted and repainted our bikes until they became truly individualized masterpieces. Reflecting on it now I realize how truly gaudy they were. Our bikes became motorcycles, cars, valiant steeds to be used jousting with fellow knights. I've owned a lot of bicycles since I've become an adult but none will ever replace that broken down, worn out piece of junk that helped carry me through childhood.

⧖

I must have walked two miles by now. Distance never seemed to matter to me when I was young. Distance then wasn't measured in feet, yards or miles; it was measured in time. How long it took to get from one experience to another. That was the real measure of distance. It's taken me thirty years to walk those two miles to the tracks. How much real distance has been traveled in that time, Jeri? Like the railroad yards, the tracks are rusty from misuse and the railroad ties are rotted with age. God, what memories these tracks hold for me. Walking on them, running alongside them. The rocks from the railroad bed, like all rocks in the area, were referred to as "doughneys" or "goonies." We hit them with sticks like baseballs, hurled them as missiles against real or imaginary enemies. The ones that glittered like crystal became diamonds. We threw them in the sewer and used them to dam up the small stream that ran along the railroad bed. They became hand grenades to be used against imaginary Japanese, German, North Korean or

Chinese enemies. Looking to the future, we also warred against the evil communist empire of Russia. We were warring little fools.

One of the things we used to do was run the ties. Stutter stepping as fast as our little feet would carry us, our eyes glued to the ties flying by, our feet seeking the unevenly spaced ties. Run until you miss but count all the while. Seeking the ultimate, a hundred straight. Miss and we started again. Great training for walking the sidewalks and avoiding the cracks, all the time the obsessive little rhyme running through our heads, "Step on a crack, break your mother's back." Yeah Jeri, "Step off a tie, break your mother's thigh." Geez, I wonder what kids had against their mothers.

Another far more challenging and much more perilous endeavor was running the rails. This was attempted only on rare occasions. I can't recall what would trigger one of these spontaneous events. Maybe our biorhythms were at a high point. More than likely, it was one of Joe Grady's impulses for self-destruction. Like lemmings heading for death, we'd follow his lead. The rails were not as wide as a balance beam and balance beams are hard to walk on, let alone try to run. Luck got you five or six steps, balance another one or two, so ten steps would get us a gymnastic score of 9.6 or 9.7. Slipping off those rails caused all kinds of injuries, most leg related but there were always exceptions.

Case in point. A kid from West Pleasant Dale was struck by one of those irresistible urges to run the rails. His name was Georgie Riley. He was about my brother Don's age. He was a good-looking kid, at least until that fateful day. Running the rails, sneakers wet, he must have been attempting a speed run. He didn't make it. Instead, he slipped and came down on the rail face first. A week later he appeared at Lenny Leed's Pool Hall. He had a pair of sunglasses on; his nose was invisible under that bandage. His front teeth, although intact, were very loose. I know that incident happened as it did because he whispered it to us through swollen, split lips. A whisper was all he could manage. The only other nose I've ever seen that badly broken was Pat Handdry's and he was hit by a car.

The ties are too rotted to walk on. Better just stick to the cinders alongside. The slate and coal piles to my left loom above me like the wall of a ravine. To my right is that huge mountain of slate, rock and low-grade coal debris. I could see it from the road, sticking high above the surrounding landscape like some large cinder cone volcano. A manmade marvel of waste, heaped up towards heaven and typical of many such mounds of the area, some much, much larger, all devoid of life. Built up of materials brought from deep within the bowels of the earth. The best and highest-grade coal was crushed, sized, washed and then loaded on coal cars. The rejected materials were carried on conveyor belts to greater and greater heights. The material was deposited at the top where it spilled down the sides creating an ever-widening base growing across as well as up. The process continued until the vein of coal beneath the surface was depleted, a process that could take years. This particular mountain was a favorite of ours. Starting at the lowest point of the base, we charged the make-believe enemies on the top. Running up was truly a Herculean feat. It was two steps forward, a step and a half back. Sneakers slid on the chunks of rock, coal and smooth slate. Charging, screaming, firing our wooden sticks that, in our minds, were BARs or rifles. A tremendous amount of time and energy were expended reaching the top. Of course, none were killed on these charges. When we played war, we were killed; that is, we fell down, counted to twenty, and got up and fought again like Lazarus risen. We didn't fall on the charges up that mountain for it was sure to cause injury. The slate was especially dangerous; it cut. Besides, the mountain has a very steep angle. Looking at it now, I realize exactly how steep it is. That was the back side; the front side facing the tracks was built up more.

As soon as I reached the tracks, I knew I was going to hike to the top. Go up the easy side, Jeri. Remember you're not nine years old anymore.

The climb to the top I know will cause me some discomfort. Probably a better way of thinking about the slight distress you'll feel, Jeri, is like the doctor telling you, "You'll feel a slight twinge of pain" as he inserted the cortisone needle into your left elbow and moved it around. Yeah, Jeri, that "slight twinge" ended up more like that small unpleasant feeling you felt when a powerful kick is delivered to a certain part of the male anatomy. The same kind of kick that could ensure that you never sired any children.

Struggling to the top for the thousandth time was not as hard as I imagined it would be. I can see quite a distance from here but I still can't see the town. The creosote plant, the railroad yards, what is left of the coal flats, the Demsey, even the area where the cemetery is located. Kind of a beautiful scene in reverse. The ugliness is just shallow, however. I can still feel the real love I have for this place, the town and those guys. Experience has taught me that effort has its rewards. I've always been interested in the outdoors, hiking, camping, climbing and running. The high one gets from the challenge, the elation one feels from reaching the top. It comes from here. It's why we did it as kids.

Attacking the mountain was just the superficial reason. The real reason, which I know now but did not think of then, was being on the top. We would be physically spent but emotionally alive. What humanists call a "peak experience."

⌛

Here I am, lying on my back, staring up at the cloudless sky. June again, summer vacation again, alive again. No car payments or rent to worry about. I'm as mentally uncluttered as I was then. I think of Joe Grady jumping off a board anchored like a diving platform into the side of the mountain. It was a good five-foot drop to the slate and rock below. A perfect cannonball dive into a waterless abyss. It was kind of difficult to tell when the cry of exhilaration changed to that of pain but change it did. Joe learned the lesson of the sand pit that day. Rock and slate is as hard as frozen sand. As Jim did the day I made my fateful leap, I jogged down to render aid to a fallen comrade. God, I wish I were nine or ten years old again.

Jim, Tucker, Joe, Sean, Spike Hollen and myself, victorious marines, now contemplating realities of our young world. Spike, a short but rugged little kid whose father owned a store, was a bit younger than us. His toughness more than bridged the age gap. Our philosophizing was cut short when Spike proclaimed, "What the shit are you guys talking about? Let's go get a Coke." To say that Spike liked Coca-Cola was akin to saying that a drug addict liked drugs. Spike loved Coke. Give him a six-pack of it and he was in heaven. We once dared him take his clothes off and run out onto Main Street at midday. He did it, but only after we chipped in and bought him a six-pack of Coke. Many in-depth conversations ended that way. Young minds wander; boredom sets in quickly and after all there are better ways to spend your time other than thinking. This is summer; school was out, ergo no thinking allowed. Save that for September. Ah Jeri, we ergoes again didn't we? Well as they say, "To *ergo* is human but to *therefore* is divine." Another Jesuitism, huh, Jeri?

⧗

Time to get up. I'm starting to get sleepy. Imagine drifting off into a deep sleep up here. Wake up after dark. Would be kind of tough to find the tracks, what with the black of coal blending with the black of night. We stayed away from here at night; it was a scary place after dark. It was even more frightening when the pale light of the full moon cast eerie shadows on bushes and piles of rock causing them to come to life.

Moonlight reflecting off the coal black surface gave a black light effect. Shadows became surrealistic. Movement seemed to slow as if I was caught in a nightmare, one from which I would not awaken. It gives me an uneasy feeling thinking of it now. I know it scared the bejesus out of me back then. Stories that circulated about strange occurrences were documented by older brothers and sisters, reinforced by nuns and parents. Stories of unholy happenings, rumors of ghosts and spirits with evil intent, of deformed human monsters who abducted those unwary children who were foolish enough to venture over those tracks at night. One such lad, intent on winning a game of hide and seek, sought the cover of the coal flats. He was never heard from again. However, no one could remember his name. He disappeared as if he had never existed so I suspect he never did. Stories like this were enough to temper the courage of even the bravest and most foolhardy among us.

Once, as a teen, I stood on the tracks, staring out across those coal flats. I could have sworn the place sprang to life; the more I looked the more I saw. Stephen King might have seen what I saw that night. Of course, I let my imagination run free. It was great material for nights when guys and girls sat together in cars on some barren road with coal dumps surrounding them trying to either make out or scare the ever loving shit out of each other, one story always topping the other.

"Time to mosey on down to the tracks, Roy." "Well all right, Gabby." It's great to be alone, talking to yourself like this. Ya never get into an argument, that's for sure. Looking down the steep side I realize why we only ran up, never down. Running up, the only thing you could do to yourself would be to fall forward and slide a little. If you ran down facing forward, you could get killed. That proves that we had some sense. The other side tapers off and not only leads to the tracks but also to a large pile of coal dirt, packed down over the years to form a somewhat solid pile of black sand. I want to see if the swallows still build nests back in those black dunes. Go ahead, Jeri, run down, after all, you did as a kid. Going down is easy, gravity takes over. Yeah, good old dependable gravity, guaranteed to flatten and scatter this aging body along the sides of this coal heap. You have to be careful, Jeri, urges you get are hard to resist. What the hell. "Geronimo. Holy shit, feet don't fail me now."

That was fun, foolhardy but fun. I guess I'm not as old as I think I am. Yeah, you're only young once, but you can be immature all your life.

🏛

There's the path. Looks like it hasn't been used in years. I want to go back to the swallows' nesting area. One of the few things I regret doing occurred here and in other spots like this one.

We were good kids. We helped stray dogs. We cared for injured birds and other animals with the possible exception of rats and snakes, and we even buried dead animals. Sometimes the exception of rats and snakes also included birds. Contradictory. BB guns, boys and birds. The old "kill the pig, kill the pig" mentality. Shooting rats with BB guns did nothing but make for a sore rat, but shoot a bird and they died. We shot birds. I still can't figure it out.

I shoot animals now, but only with a camera. I'm not against hunting. I've seen deer starved by overpopulation after a hard winter. I just don't hunt. I don't like guns and maybe that's why. I know how to use them, been taught by experts. I remember when I stopped shooting birds. I picked one up and felt its little heart stop beating in my hand. It was a little sparrow. I didn't kill it to eat it or in self-defense. I killed it for sport. I never shot a bird after that. We did shoot rats with .22's when I was a teen; they were vermin, but I don't think I would do it now. Funny how we all change.

The nests are still there. Complete with the birds. The way they flew always reminded me of a jet fighter, sleek and fast. Their scythe-shaped wings allow them to turn, twist, roll like a stunt plane in an air show. We were never able to hit one and I'm glad of it. What a waste it would have been. We used to target practice with BB guns here. Probably why we started to shoot at the swallows. One day in particular pops into my mind. Tucker Breslin's brother Joe and I were here. Joe had a real bow and practice arrows, not the kind of bows we used to make out of saplings. This one probably was about a 35 lb. pull bow. Joe made what I thought was a kind of ordinary comment, "Watch this." He drew the bow back and then all of a sudden pointed it straight up in the air and let go of the arrow. Now, I'm not a rocket scientist or anything like that but I knew something Joe had not thought of while performing his spontaneous act. What goes up must come down. I think I took the Lord's name in vain, followed by a quick Act of Contrition. The arrow was out of sight. Joe's facial expression changed. My bowels felt loose for I thought I was about to do the unthinkable: die with dirty underwear on. Even when the arrow fell to earth it seemed invisible. Just a sudden and sobering thud, probably less than a foot and a half from us. As calmly as I could, I asked him why the hell he did that. No answer, just that puzzled look on his face, staring through me as if to say, "Why the hell did I do that?" He just shook his head and never really answered me. I understood. How can you possibly explain an impulse?

I can't see the top from this angle; I can't even see the tracks. This place is a natural shooting range. Once Joe Grady and I snuck his uncle John's souvenir Japanese army rifle out of Joe's house along with some ammo. Like the way we smuggled a lot of things out of his house, I'd hide under the bushes and he'd pass it out the upstairs window to me and we'd take off. We'd do the same thing to put it back.

What a thrill. We both got to shoot it. This was another one of those "we could have killed ourselves" episodes. I wonder how we got through childhood alive. Great fun!

Better get back to the tracks. You've dilly-dallied here long enough, young man. Now get a move on. God, it's great to be able to talk to yourself. Not necessarily the most intelligent conversation I ever had, however.

Looking back at the mountain from the tracks I know how much that place helped build me. Physically, the running up it as a child strengthened my body; as a teen I used it to condition myself for football. Psychologically, it strengthened my resolve to work, to achieve, attain the top, mind over body. Hard as it got for me at times, I stuck to it.

⧗

As I move on to Polack Hill, the coal dumps decrease in size. Dumps to my left, coal flats to my right, Polack Hill in the distance.

Polack Hill is a place where many battles occurred. Most friendly, but rough. Polack Hill is the name we used to describe the part of town inhabited by Polish immigrants and their descendants. No disrespect was ever meant by using the word "Polack." It was an expression, like West Pleasant Dale or any other word used as slang in the area. We went to school with the kids that lived on the hill. We played with them. We liked them but we fought with them. Even now I don't know why. There never really was any animosity between us.

Rock fights. We used to throw rocks at each other. We'd gather at the bottom or in the middle of the hill. They positioned themselves at the top if we occupied the middle or the middle if we were at the bottom. Words were exchanged and the battle commenced. There were rules, unwritten of course, but rules nonetheless. They were simple: no slate. Slate was flat and sharp. It traveled further and was hard to see. Getting hit with slate was not fun. Getting hit with one of those railroad bedrocks was no fun either. Being heavy, they never attained great speed; being large, they were easy to spot and evade. Usually none of us suffered any real injury. Oh, you might accidentally get a goose egg but that was rare because there was never any real malice intended. We lobbed rocks up at them and they'd return the lobs. Battles were short and both sides usually retreated unharmed.

There is always of course that rare exception. A kid by the name of Bobby Lester was with us one day. He didn't normally play with us. He just happened to be around the neighborhood hanging out. Bobby had been in an accident about three weeks before. It happened at lunchtime in back of St. Marie's Grade School. Bobby was running around the corner of the school. It just so happened he ran into a girl's softball game in progress. Now I mean he literally ran into it. It seems his head arrived at the plate slightly before the softball did. Maggie Kearn was at full swing and unable to stop. It would have been a solid single except Bobby intercepted the bat before the ball did. I forget the number of stitches required to close the area above his left eye, but it was a lot. He spent some time in the hospital.

Anyway, Bobby joined us in play the first active day he'd seen since the accident. Our powers of persuasion convinced him to join us in combat. We were attacking the hill. "Don't worry, Bobby, nobody ever gets hurt. Besides, it's a lot of fun." He believed us, mainly because we believed us. After all, no one really got hurt in these mock battles. We massed at the bottom, about eight of us against about an equal number of the "enemy." After exchanging a few "Your mommas wear combat boots," and "Oh yeahs," the charge began. We were met with the usual barrage. We, of course, returned fire. All was proceeding as usual when to my left I heard a loud scream. I looked over. There was Bobby, rolling around on the ground, holding on to his now re-injured head. I remember thinking to myself, "Hey, isn't that where he got hit before?" He was covered with blood. It scared the shit out of him and the rest of us.

He got up, running in place, holding the left side of his head. He suddenly put it in gear and took off. We didn't see him for a while. The scar on his face was a lot uglier the second time around. He told us his mother absolutely, positively forbid him to play with us again. Too bad, he was a nice kid. Oh well, it happens.

There's the gap between the coal dumps and Polack Hill. Trees, plants and all kinds of neat things occupy the little stretch of no man's land. The path that leads through it to the old breaker has long since disappeared, overgrown from years of disuse. Occasionally a group of us used to travel through that little stretch of woods to play in the old breaker. It reminded me of an old castle. When we played there, we were always in danger of the Polish kids catching us. Now this was cause for real conflict. No mock battles there. A real fight would ensue. After all, it was their domain. We'd keep a sharp eye out for them. If we spotted them, we'd beat a hasty retreat for we were sure to be greatly outnumbered.

One day Spike Hollen, Joe Grady and I went on our search for the "holy grail." We found the "castle," deserted as usual. We stormed the gate, which actually was an old pathway for a conveyor belt, breaching the walls that consisted of a rotted out fence-like structure meant to keep the workers from falling off the breaker. We immediately headed for the "dungeons." The dungeons were two deep v-shaped upside down triangles meant to hold coal until it was released into coal trucks below. Once inside the dungeons, the real fun began. The rusted out metal sides offered a genuine chance for the unwary to be struck down with tetanus, the dreaded lockjaw. Visions of being unable to talk, being unable to answer any of Sister Bertha's questions, then suffering the consequences of such disrespect, that was the real dread from lockjaw, not death. Of course, we were the "unwary." Now I never met anyone who had lockjaw nor had I ever met anyone who ever met anyone who had contracted this deadly disease. It was probably just a ploy put out by the adult world to limit the young much like the "Don't swim after eating" warning.

Getting back to the dungeons. Entering them was no problem; we just slid down. Getting out was another story. They were very steep sided. Once on the bottom, we'd have to run up the other side, each time getting closer and closer to the top. This took effort, of course. Each time we'd get out, we'd slide back down. After about four escapes, lactic acid started to build up in the muscles. Each escape became more and more challenging. Sooner or later we were bound to run out of gas. Knowing this we'd toss down a board to be used as a ladder when our bodies gave out. About seven escapes was tops. The eighth would always end up short. We'd be there sweating like racehorses, gulping air, enjoying our vision quest. We'd hoist ourselves out for the final time and head home. This was our normal routine. We were creatures of habit. This, of course, was known not only by us but also by the kids from Polack Hill.

On the day in question, Joe, Spike and I headed home. We made our way out unobserved or so we thought. Reaching the tracks, which was always neutral territory, spirits high, bodies rust covered and spent, our gait slowed. No need to hurry. Just walking along shooting the shit. Another raid, another success. Chalk one up for the good guys, the guys in the rust colored outfits. It doesn't get any better than this. General George Armstrong Custer was probably thinking the same thing at Little Big Horn. Just then Spike made one of his pointed comments. "Holy shit, let's get the hell out of here!" I looked over at his passing shoulder. There on top of the hill walking parallel to us were about eight kids, not friendly ones either. Our one hope was an all-out sprint to a narrow path at the bottom of Polack Hill, then fifty yards beyond the path where we'd be home free. They wouldn't dare follow us up Blackthorne Street; they'd be outnumbered. We were outdistancing them. Spike and I were neck and neck, Joe was only slightly to our rear and slowing. We were going to make it. "What the hell?" Joe slowed. They started to catch up to him. "Come on, Joe," Spike and I yelled words of encouragement over our shoulders. Then he did something that to this day I've never been able to figure out. He turned around and tackled the lead kid. They swarmed over him like flies on a manure pile. Spike and I stopped, dumbfounded. We had no choice; we had to go back as a matter of honor. That idiot did it again. One thing Joe didn't lack was courage. Wisdom, maybe, but not courage. This was to be a beating that I wouldn't forget for a long time. Spike and I launched ourselves into the fray. Diving on a bunch of bodies rolling over and over then coming to rest. There was a kid on each of my arms. Stosh Bednzi straddled me, his hand cupped over my nose and mouth. I was struggling for breath; none was coming. Then out of the corner of my eye, I saw Spike free a pinned arm. He reached out, grabbed a rock and hit the kid on top of him in the head. Partially free, he rolled over the top of the other kid holding him down and nailed him in the head also. On his feet, Spike pulled Stosh off me. My nose and mouth were free, breathing in precious gulps of air. I freed an arm. Rolling over, getting hit. All seemed hazy. I don't know how long we fought. We were, however, not beating the odds. The odds in this case—the Polish kids—were tiring themselves out on our battered and bruised bodies. They finally let us go, warning us not to return if we knew what was good for us, which of course, we didn't.

When we got back to our neighborhood, the other guys wanted revenge. Spike, Joe and I wanted to forget. The incident passed as so many did. As they say, what goes around comes around. Their turn would come sooner or later.

Looking up to my left, Polack Hill seems to fold over me like a warm comforter on a brisk fall evening. Just remembering that lost battle brings a smile to my face. Spike saving my butt. Joe, who was not an exceptional fighter, standing his ground. Me, wanting to run, but knowing I couldn't. It was all so clear back then. Only right and wrong, no gray in between. We were wrong being over there, just as they would have been wrong if they invaded our castles. We would have reacted the same. We were right to stand and aid a friend.

Another not quite so normal day of play rests firmly in my memory, as I reach the path to Blackthorne Street. The street looks different, more modern and paved now, not the brick that gave it a cobblestone effect. It's blacktop. Pleasant Dale has moved into the future. More houses. People built houses all the way down here. I feel like going back to the tracks. The only change there occurred from aging. Well, Jeri, nothing lasts forever.

I can't even tell where the sewer used to be. God I hope they filled that in. No one told us to stay away from the sewer. I guess they figured we wouldn't be dumb enough to play near an open sewer. Geez, that place stunk. We'd sit on the railroad tracks and look down into it. We knew every time someone flushed his or her toilet. We'd see a rush of water followed by another brown trout en route to the Demsey. Toilet paper dissolving in water gave it the appearance of a white morass. I saw my first prophylactic swimming downstream out the pipe from below that bricked street. One of the older guys said it was a rubber, but I knew that wasn't true because rubbers were something you slipped on over your shoes to keep your feet from getting wet in the rain. It was a very strange looking balloon. One kid said his dad had a drawer full of them at home. He said they came individually wrapped which seemed like a real waste of paper. After all, Lenny Leed sold them by the handful for just a few pennies and they were much more colorful than that white piece of rubber we saw that day.

The sewer was a fascinating place for us. There were rats there. We could throw rocks into its ash-like waters then count the seconds it took for them to sink. This we did on extremely boring days. The overflow from the sewer ran through a tunnel underneath the railroad tracks. A small stream blended in with sewer water and eventually made its way to the mighty Demsey.

Crossing over the railroad tracks was absolutely forbidden. We took this order rather seriously because violation meant swift and sure punishment. One of the older guys taught us how to beat this ban, and beat it honestly. All we had to do was get into the tunnel, which was no small feat in itself, hold our breath and run, hunchback style, underneath the tracks. We didn't cross over them so you actually were not disobeying. This was not a pleasant way of getting to the black paradise across the tracks but it was effective.

Not one of us who ever made this "great escape" got away scot-free. There was a penalty to be paid and pay you did. The first time a soggy, wet, rubber-bottomed sneaker came in contact with partially dissolved human excrement, was a time to be remembered. The odor stayed with you all day, or at least until your mom accused you of doing "doo-doo" in your pants. We did the tunnel many times until we finally realized it just wasn't worth the effort.

Disobeying was a sin, and we all knew it, but we figured it was one of those venial ones, the kind of sin that only slightly soiled your soul, not the mortal kind that called for eternal damnation. Confession would wipe it out and at a mere cost of three and three, i.e. three Our Father's and three Hail Mary's—a piece of cake. We'd just walk down the tracks then under cover of Polack Hill straight across the three sets of tracks.

The sewer was approachable, and approach we did. If you were looking from the tracks there was a huge crab-apple tree to the right of the sewer and an open space to the left. That apple tree grew well in its fertile habitat and its large spreading branches drooped to form a canopy. Many an hour was whiled away in that make-believe "hole in the wall," our hideout. Away from prying eyes, we discussed, planned, fantasized. Outlaws or good guys, it mattered not what we were, we were having fun. Joe Grady used to swipe a pack of Luckies from his mother's carton of cigarettes, throw them out the window and we'd be off. Galloping on our make-believe steeds, we'd clippity-clop our way to the hideout, there to smoke our ill-gotten loot. Lighting up and puffing our little heads off, getting that foul tasting smoke in our mouths, hacking and coughing if we accidentally inhaled. We had no idea what inhaling was, thank God. When all twenty cigarettes were properly disposed of, we'd chuck the empty pack into the sewer. Getting rid of the telltale smell of tobacco from our breaths was just a matter of eating a couple of handfuls of Sen-Sens, purchased from Lenny Leed's in advance of our robbery.

On one such occasion, all the Breslins joined us: Joe, Chuckie, Bobby and Billy, along with a bunch of us who had just finished a pack of Luckies. We all walked over to the sewer to dispose of the evidence. All of a sudden we heard a kind of splash, more like a splock, followed by a cry for help. Billy Breslin had done the unthinkable: he slipped and fell into the sewer. He was followed by his brother Chuck who jumped in to save him. Not to be outdone, Joe jumped in to save both of them. By now all three were in deep shit, so to speak. Joe Grady and Jim McAndrews ran for rope. I yelled encouragement. Bobby and Tucker joined their brothers, each trying to save the one before. They were slowly sinking the way bad guys sank in quicksand in the movies. Those of us standing there watching liked the Breslin brothers but we saw no point in joining them in the sewer. Slipping and sliding, they were getting nowhere fast. They say shit happens. I guess it does. Help finally arrived just in the nick of time, at least that was the case for Billy. Being the smallest, he sank almost to his head. The rope was cast and one by one we retrieved the Breslins from their shitty plight.

None of the Breslins were seen for days after this episode. Mr. and Mrs. Breslin were not extremely fond of their sons chosen swimming hole. Now you might think we made fun of them when we did see them again, but we didn't. We knew it took courage to jump into that sewer to save a brother. Plus, it could have been any one of us in there, so the incident at the sewer was over but not really forgotten. We learned from it, another step toward maturity. A small one I might add.

⧗

Blackthorne Street. How many times I rode, ran, rattled and roared down this once bricked hill. It really is a series of three hills. One ran above Main Street to the traffic light. Another ended in front of our house where the street leveled off for a few hundred yards. The third and most thrilling of all started at St. Marie's, the Irish Catholic church of our town, and ended in front of a large oak tree that was located about one hundred and fifty yards from the sewer. A dirt road formed a right angle to the street and continued up and over Polack Hill. From feet, to wheels, to sleighs, we ambled, coasted, slid or flew like bolts of lightning down these inclines. The first time I ever had my bell rung happened when sleigh and tree collided, with my head acting as a bumper for the sleigh.

One of our favorite pastimes was building soapbox racers. The whole gang of us would scrounge up old wheels from doll or baby carriages, combine them with wood, rope and orange crates to create a racer. We'd traverse the lower hill in front of the church. Careening along at breathtaking speeds, bouncing off curbs and each other, we'd race our little hearts out until every last racer was returned to its original condition: scrap. We'd gather up our junk and return to our backyards, where working in teams like the finest NASCAR pit crews, we'd rebuild our dismantled horseless chariots and be ready to go again. No one was ever injured in these events. Turtles passed us on the way down the hill, but we didn't care. We were racers, bound for glory, but not for Akron, Ohio, where the soapbox derby finals are held.

On bikes we'd build up speed, then halfway down the last hill slam on the brakes and slide into the street that paralleled the side of the Gradys' house. Many a game of touch football was played on the flat area between my house and the church, our running and passing interrupted periodically by a passing car. These games caused injury to most of us at one time or another. Sprained ankles, bumps, bruises and brush burns were the most common. Running out for a pass with our eyes riveted on the ball, we'd momentarily forget the curbing that bordered the street on both sides. This was the major source of damage to our persons. These games were serious events but not nearly as serious as our tackle football games, which were, to say the least, rough and tumble. Then there were the dashes. Uphill sprints, downhill sprints, flat-out races. We used the hill in front of the church to sleigh ride down, but only occasionally. Usually we sledded a different area because too much traffic made the church hill too dangerous.

The Grady house, remodeled now, has a housemate. It's built on the field to the side. That was a playing field for us. We made a baseball diamond there. The only problem was the outfield. It was overgrown and a good four feet lower than the infield. This really didn't matter much. We had so many kids playing it was nearly impossible to get the ball past everyone. We couldn't hit a homer because of the ball we used. We never played with a new ball; we never had a new ball. Our baseballs had long since lost their covers. Replacing the covers was no real big deal because of electrical tape, that black sticky tape used on wires. It was so sticky we had to roll the ball in ashes so we could throw it. Some of the baseballs took on massive proportions. I've often wondered if we cut one of them in half and counted the layers of tape if we'd get the same effect as counting the rings of a fallen tree to assess its age. These balls and bats passed, as the bicycles and sleighs did, from brother to brother. The bats, like the balls, were repaired over and over again. Cracked bats, nailed and glued, were covered with tape, rubbed with ashes and ready for use. The weight of the ball, and the give of the bat, made for very shallow hits. There was one exception, one that made me rethink my desire to play the national pastime.

Jim McAndrews was pitching; a kid by the name of Tommy O'Keefe was batting. Tommy was a large, powerful kid. He appeared to be fat. This was deceptive. (I learned this firsthand one day when I dared him to punch me in the arm. He did and it hurt. Another lesson well learned.) Jim wound up and delivered a fastball or about as fast as it would go. Tommy hit it. Hard. The crack of the bat was followed by another sound, a sickening thud. Jim got hit square in the face. Blood literally flew out of his nose. Jim just stood there stunned, then realizing what happened, he let out a scream of pain. He ran up the alley and home. I felt sorry for him. He was my best friend but a deeper feeling came over me, one of fear. I wasn't all that fearful of playing baseball before that incident, but all that changed. I never cared for the game after that. As a matter of fact, I don't like it even now.

⧗

You better move out of the middle of the street, Jeri. What will the neighbors think? Words to that effect seem inappropriate now. The Grady house, the trees between the house and the area where the field used to be are gone. Now geez, those trees. Four young maples with straight limber trunks, and the granddaddy of all maples on the corner of the line sired all of them. We'd climb those trees, light and limber like the little monkeys that we were. Once at the top, we started swaying back and forth as if they were some amusement park ride. Luckily, those trees were sturdier than we were smart.

Joe Grady, that daring, foolhardy adventurer, once challenged the big one. This patriarch of all maples would not be tampered with. Our daring young climber reached that point where the tree, like the witch in *Hansel and Gretel,* snared its prey. Joe looked down, a no-no in the climbing world. Frozen in place, hands holding fast like magnets on a refrigerator door, Joe met his match. His Uncle John tried every trick he knew to talk him down, all to no avail. Joe would not be moved. It took engine number nine, four volunteer firemen and a frantic mother praying the rosary to lower Joe from this lofty perch. Geez, what a day.

44

Joe never had much luck with trees. There was a nice-sized tree along the back of his house. One hot August afternoon we were busying ourselves picking apples. Joe, out on a limb so to speak, lost his balance and fell. When we got to him, he was unconscious. Now we didn't really know the difference between unconsciousness and death. After repeatedly slapping his face, looking under his eyelids, raising his arm only to have it fall limply back to the ground, we concluded Joe was now either in heaven, hell or purgatory depending on his last confession. Spike, Jim, Sean and I ran to the Gradys' back door. Knocking as hard as we could, we finally got Mrs. Grady's attention. Mrs. Grady was not a well woman. She had a heart condition. Mrs. Grady inquired about Joe's absence since he was the only one not present. We broke the news with all the compassion our ages would allow. "Mrs. Grady, Joe's dead; he fell out of the apple tree on his head." Her face turned the color of vanilla ice cream and she started to gasp for air. About this time, we were joined by a very groggy Joe who was complaining loudly about a fierce headache. I don't know if Mrs. Grady ever really felt the same towards us after that day. Thinking of Joe now, the term "death wish" comes to mind.

⧗

I remember standing by the father maple talking to Jim McAndrews. It was the kind of day we clustered in small groups, not playing, not planning, just running on idle, I guess. There were a couple of kids from one of the other neighborhoods hanging out with us. A kid by the name of Joe Dillion had a milk bottle. Like a lot of things back then, milk was delivered to your door by the local dairy. These bottles were heavy, reusable containers built to last. They were kind of neat, especially in the winter when it was so cold the milk froze, forcing the top layer of cream out over the sides. Packaging back then, before the Chicago Tylenol problems, was different. Things were easy to open. No one ever dreamed of poisoning his or her fellow man for fun. You're drifting again, Jeri. Focus the mind; get to the point before you forget the point. Talking to yourself again, great.

Well anyway, Joe Dillion was trying to organize a football game using the bottle as a football. My family never really credited me with superior intelligence, and thinking back over my earlier years, I'd have to agree with them, but I knew playing football with a milk bottle was stupid. Just think, falling onto a bottle after being tackled would be hazardous to your health. Jim and I voiced our opinion on the issue and continued doing what we were doing, which was nothing. All of a sudden, I heard my nickname, "Doc." I turned around but not fast enough to get my hands up. Joe Dillion threw me a pass that I caught with my face, or to be more precise, my nose. I can't explain the feeling, a pain, dull yet sharp. The only way I can describe this kind of pain from being hit in the nose is by telling someone to imagine sliding down a banister, then have the banister turn into a razor blade.

Of the four times I broke my nose, this was the first. They say you never forget the first time. Somehow I don't think they were referring to breaking your nose. Well, I never forgot either.

Thinking about football, bottles, pains, et cetera, reminds me of my first black eye. Playing football on the field one day I went in for a tackle. Next thing I know I'm holding my head. My brother Don was there. He pried my hands away from my head and then I realized I was blind in my right eye. I couldn't see. "Holy shit," I started to cry. Don laughed, "You idiot, you got a black eye. It's just swollen shut." Pain changed to exhilaration. I got a black eye! Yeah, all right, way to go, Jeri! Can't wait to get to school tomorrow to show it off.

The only real drawback about noticeable injuries was Mom. Mom had no sense of humor when it came to injuries, especially after she found out you were going to live. Best die from the injury. That way you'd get a lot less grief from your mom. All the guys' moms took life too seriously when it came to their children.

⧗

Better move on; don't want to stay in one place too long. There doesn't seem to be anyone around. No kids. There are no kids here. Unreal. Up the street on the left was the Finagins' house. Now they had kids. Nine, I think. More boys than girls, if I remember right. Their dad worked for the government in Pittston. Like all the families around here, they were very active in the church. An alley ran between their house and the rectory. The church stood next to the rectory. Across the street from the church were the Murphys' and the Sweeneys' houses. The Murphys had two boys, both about my brothers' ages. I wonder who lives in these houses now.

I'm stopping at St. Marie's. I haven't been in there in more years than I care to remember. The church was the fabric of our lives. Church, school, home. All were so important to us. The religion molded us, our families taught us its values. God, the sisters and priests, our mothers and fathers, our brothers and sisters, our neighbors: "Love them as they love you. Respect all people, places and things."

Even today I don't care how much younger a priest or nun is than I am, I still call them Father or Sister out of respect for who they are, what they stand for. My mom's younger brother, my uncle, was Father Nilus. His real name was Francis, yet I never heard her address him as anything other than Father. Even my grandmother called her own son Father. I know Mom wanted one of us boys to become a priest, the ultimate for an Irish-Catholic family at the time.

The outside of the church has changed somewhat; it's got new doors. Just walking up these steps is a walk back into time for me. I was an altar boy from third grade all the way through my senior year in high school. I entered church more by the sacristy door than I did by the front door. Mom would go to Mass early during the week. If one of the altar boys didn't show up, she'd come home and wake me up. I served an awful lot of Masses. The inside seems different; pews, confessionals, the Stations of the Cross are the same but the altar has changed. Years ago the priest faced away from the parishioners, the Mass was said in Latin, the altar boys responded in Latin. Sitting here in the back, the church is dark and deserted. I have kind of an eerie feeling. The candles flicker in front of the statue of the Virgin Mary. Those are the little candles we lit when we had a special intention. Many a nickel and dime I put in there. I had a lot of intentions. Some dealt with Christmas presents; others were for cloudless summer days.

One in particular was a plea to Jesus, Mary and Joseph to soften Sister Bertha's heart and keep her from calling

Mom. Mom really had an Irish temper. When it came to her children and school, she not only had a temper; she had no sense of humor. That particular intention was not answered. I vividly remember sitting on the couch putting on my sneakers. The phone rang. No big deal. See, I really thought Jesus, Mary and Joseph were going to come through for me. Mom answered the phone, then turned her head towards me, her face reddened. This was not a good sign from a first generation Irish woman. Then her words that confirmed my worst fears. "He did what?" Oh dear God, am I in deep doo-doo. No use running, I only had one sneaker on. Besides, that would just make her madder. Now my mind was racing. See, I really didn't do anything, but Sister Bertha swore I did. Wrongly accused, I really counted on that candle, honesty as the best policy, et cetera. Now, I was desperate. I whipped off a fast, silent prayer to St. Jude, patron saint of lost causes. No help there either. Mom placed the phone in its cradle, a wild look in her eye. Oh dear God, I'm dead. For a short, stocky woman she covered the distance to the couch in a split second. Too late for me to react. My last desperate plea, "Ma, I didn't do it." Her reply makes sense to me now, but not then. "I don't care, you've done plenty you haven't been caught for." Perfect logic for my mom. She was all over me, the verbal tongue lashing far worse than the physical beating now being administered, no mercy, no let up. I remember a statement she kept uttering. "Don't tell me, I raised two boys before you." There was no such thing back then as being held in double jeopardy. Punished by Sister Bertha meant the phone call, punishment by Mom, followed by those oft spoken words, "Wait till your father gets home."

Poor Pop. He really worked physically hard. Upon arriving home he was now faced with the problem of his errant son. I remember this particular day as if it happened yesterday. I was really scared. Pop never really hit any one of us except my brother Don, but then again Don really tested the patience of the saints. He'd get in trouble, knowing he was going to get in trouble and he'd still go out and get in trouble. Pop hit me with a newspaper one day for running across the street; other than that, he never physically punished me. He was physically very strong but it wasn't that I feared. It was his little one-on-one reminders about behavior. Those little one-way heart-to-heart talks. Well, this day Mom proceeded to describe in secondhand detail, Sister Bertha's account of my dastardly deed. Pop listened frowning. Pop called me into the kitchen. Mom left. Pop shut the door, not a good sign for me. "Sit down, Jeri." I sat muted. He looked me in the eye. "Jeri, take it easy on your mother, understand?" I nodded; he nodded. That was it. I was off the hook. Maybe he figured the wrath of Sister Bertha, followed by Mom's, was enough. Jesus, Mary and Joseph, with the help of St. Jude, came through for me. It could have been a lot worse. My intention was partially granted and therefore it fit in with the divine will of God the nuns always talked about.

⌛

The confessionals are a little more modernized than I remember. Looking at them reminds me of my first Holy Communion. For Catholics this is an important day. It's on par with Baptism and Confirmation. The day before you received your First Communion you had to make your First Confession. Many hours of practice went into learning those words. "Bless me Father for I have sinned" followed by "It's been (fill in the time) since my last confession." Well, I went to confession. Mom was so proud she told me to go up to Fallon's Store and get myself a treat. I chose an orange creamsicle. Boy was it good. The orange ice surrounding the vanilla ice cream all fastened on a popsicle stick. It tasted so good I charged another to Mom's bill. Mr. Fallow must have got suspicious, and when I left he called my mom, or at least that's what I think happened. I arrived home. Mom was sitting on the front porch, not really unusual for a Saturday afternoon. "Jeri, did you have a creamsicle?" "Yeah, Ma." "Jeri, did you have more than one creamsicle?" Uh, oh. My underarms started to sweat. "Ah." "Did you Jeri?" "Yes, Ma." "You just finished your first confession and then you stole a creamsicle. Well young man, march yourself back to confession. You stole and that's a sin."

That walk down the block to the church was one of the longest I've ever made in my life. I was careful crossing the street, for to get hit by a car and die with this horrible atrocity on my soul would mean eternal damnation. As I took my place in line, the fear and shame was overwhelming. What would Father Cornelius say? I was sweating up a storm by now. My turn arrived; reluctantly I entered the confessional. Tension mounted as I waited for the small door next to Father Cornelius's head to open. It happened so quickly, I thought I was going to do a number one in my pants. My voice was quaking, "Bless me Father for I have sinned. It's been twenty minutes since my last confession." My voice cracked tearfully. I sobbed my version of the story. I was sure I'd have to say the rosary every day for the next twenty years.

Funny thing, I think Father was so mortified by my sin he was crying along with me. He had a funny way of crying. It almost sounded like my Pop when he was laughing really hard. My story ended; there was dead silence. He was probably trying to compose himself, maybe thinking of some words to express his outrage at my wanton disregard for my mother and all that was holy. What seemed like minutes passed, Father's voice still had an edgy quality to it. He was so stunned all he said was, "Well, Jeri, please try to be better in the future." Even more surprising was my penance. One Our Father, one Hail Mary and one Glory Be to the Father; not much considering the severity of the sin. My guardian angel probably put in a good word for me.

Confessions were a weekly ritual for all of us. Every Saturday afternoon, without fail we found ourselves in that long line waiting to cleanse our souls. The nuns always likened our soul to a milk bottle. After confession it was rich and white, full of purity and brightness. Then every time we committed a slight transgression, better known to us as a venial sin, a small speck of dirt would taint the purity of our milk. As we racked up more and more venial sins, our milk bottle would become clustered with dots of black marks. This however was not real cause for concern for us. It just lengthened our time in purgatory. A mortal sin, one that called for eternal damnation, this was really cause for alarm. Our milk bottle turned completely black with sin, an ugly image as pictured in the Baltimore Catechism. This was real serious. Eternity is a long time. We were always told that eternity was like a sparrow flying to the top of Mt. Everest and removing a small pebble then returning a hundred years later and removing another pebble. This would be repeated until Mt. Everest was as flat as a pancake. That was just the first day. This coupled with the fact that you were boiling in a pot of oil all this time.

Now some confessions were easy. "Bless me Father for I have sinned. It's been one week since my last confession." Then, "I disobeyed five times, I swore twice," et cetera. But then life became more complicated. I got older; sex sprung to life and reared its ugly head. Now I entered the world of thought, deeds and occasions for sins. Life was complicated enough with just disobeying, lying and an occasional curse thrown in. The length of time necessary to explain the complexities of my offenses increased. People looked at me as I came out of confession after eight minutes as if "I'd like to know what that kid did." Lectures often accompanied a particularly complicated week of sinning.

No matter how much I disguised my voice Father Cornelius would just say, "Jeri, do you have a cold?" Darn, he knew. Our lives when we were younger were relatively simple. Our reasoning led us to the conclusion that if we died immediately after confession, we'd go to heaven. Oh, we might spend time in purgatory, but heaven was assured. No boiling in oil while waiting for some sparrow to flatten Mt. Everest.

Leaving confessions we often ran headlong across the street without looking, knowing if we got hit by a car all our bases were covered. Our soul was pure as a bottle of milk and we had clean underwear on. We'd go to heaven and our moms wouldn't be embarrassed because of our undergarments. When we became teenagers, we'd head up to the Polish Catholic Church, St. James and John's. One priest spoke very little English therefore confessions were somewhat less embarrassing for us.

One of the things I really like about the church is the feeling of oneness I get when I'm there all by myself. Silent prayer. The feeling God is giving you His undivided attention.

The choir loft was where the parish choir sang those beautiful Gregorian hymns. Those chants that were so uplifting, so moving. The choir loft was a mysterious place. From that vantage point you were able to see all but the very last row of pews. The sensation was one of being in heaven looking down.

For me, the real heart of the church building was its bells. They were found above the choir loft. A door concealed the steps that took you to the bell tower. I can remember accompanying Mr. McAndrews and Jim up those narrow and foreboding steps to ring the bells for the Angeles. The bells tolled at 6:00 A.M., at noon and at 6:00 P.M. Mr. McAndrews would let Jim and I ring one. We'd hang on to the rope. With all our might we'd give it a tug to get the bell ringing. Once you got it in motion the weight of the bell made it easy to continue. The harder of the two bells Mr. McAndrews would toll. His large, powerful arms straining, the bells would sound, calling all the faithful to the prayer, the Angeles. When Jim and I got bigger, he'd let us go by ourselves to ring the bells. If we climbed the ladder up to the bells, we could look out and see a good portion of the neighborhood.

Winter nights were particularly memorable. The bell tower took on a macabre appearance. Only a small dim bulb lit the stairwell; its glow illuminated the platform you stood on to pull the ropes. The chill from the winter's evening, the darkness of the early night, seemed to amplify sounds from the church itself. The spirits of the saints were sure to dwell within. We could imagine the souls of all the faithfully departed filling the pews to celebrate the Mass of the Dead. Our active little minds envisioned those and many more scenes. We did not linger long at our tasks these nights. It was up the steps, ring the bell and get the heck out.

On good days, after we finished, we'd stop at the church's huge pipe organ. We'd take turns pretending to play the instrument. It really was a joy to hear the organ being played by an expert. For weddings, funerals and feast days the music fit the occasion.

As an altar boy, I spent many hours tending to one task or another. On Good Friday, I'd volunteer to kneel in front of the altar for all three hours that Christ hung on the cross. Two altar boys were always present during this time, kneeling erect, ignoring their discomfort, knowing it was nothing compared to the agony on the cross. I'd spend hours racking up indulgences; reducing the time I'd have to spend in purgatory. I was informed later that these could not be used for one's self but had to be applied to others who had since departed this earth. I sure knocked off a lot of time for some dear departed soul.

The sign of the cross was worth three years. If you used holy water it was worth seven, but you had to follow it up with an Our Father, a Hail Mary or a Glory Be to the Father. I usually used the Glory Be, because you could say a lot of them in a short period of time. If you recited the Angeles at dawn, noon and at eventide, you received ten years for each time. Do it a month straight and you received a plenary indulgence, which is a full remission of sin. The Divine Praises, if said privately, were worth three years. Recite them publicly and they were worth five years. I tried one Good Friday to keep count of all the days and years I was accumulating. I was doing a great job of addition until Father Cornelius motioned for me to kneel up straight. Well, I lost count, almost cursed to myself, and then feeling so bad about that, I suffered pangs of conscience. I had to ask Father Cornelius if thinking of cursing was the same as cursing. He looked at me, shook his head and asked me, "Why?" "Oh nothing," I said. Best let it ride, no use pushing the near occasion of sin angle too far. I might actually find out what it really meant.

Even if I did not kneel at the altar on Good Friday, I still went to church and observed those three hours of silence. Holy Week meant Lent was about over. That lessened our fish intake by one day a week. We not only abstained from meat on Fridays but also on Wednesdays during Lent. Just thinking about all the fish I ate in my lifetime turns my stomach. Fish may be the healthiest of foods, but to me it meant creamed codfish on mashed potatoes, which I liberally covered with pepper. This was our mainstay on Fridays until Mom discovered Mrs. Paul's frozen fish sticks. That dish, coupled with baked French fries, could be liberally coated with ketchup. For me, Mrs. Paul provided a change from a somewhat predictable weekly menu.

Easter time also meant smoked kielbasa. This was the real thing, purchased in the basement of St. James and John's Polish Catholic Church. This was a taste treat, fried with eggs and home fries for breakfast or cut lengthwise and fried to make great sandwiches. I rarely ever find its equal today.

The basement of the Polish church also held other treats. Stuffed cabbage, or as we called it "pigs in the blanket," stuffed green peppers, bread dough with cheese in the middle deep fried, Polish hams, and floured mashed potatoes with cheese in the middle, likewise fried to a golden brown. Today a cardiac specialist's nightmare, that bill of fare is definitely not recommended by the American Heart Association. The Polish people in town raised a lot of money for their church selling these goodies to the Irish people; the Irish were not noted for their culinary talents.

Christmas at the church was also a festive time of year. Of all things Christmas means to children—the anticipation, the tree, Santa Claus, the presents, no school, our visits to the church to see the Baby Jesus in the manger— the thing I looked forward to most was becoming old enough to go to Midnight Mass. It was a crossover period. We got our feet into the adult world.

There were customs we followed: Mom's boiling chicken all day so we could have chicken rice soup after Midnight Mass, having oyster soup which we ate for Christmas Eve meal and placing a candle in the window welcoming any stranger who could not be home for Christmas.

That candle was not just for show. Pop actually took in two young soldiers who were hitchhiking home for Christmas but would never make it. He picked them up on his way home from work. We fed them, took them to church, put them up for the night and got them on their way early Christmas morning. Pop and Mom were generous people. Francis, my oldest brother, missed three Christmases while stationed in Japan. I know these young GIs reminded us how much we missed Fran.

Come Christmas Eve with snow falling, off to Mass we'd go. The beauty of the service, the warmth of friends and family, the choir never sounding better. I can feel tears welling up inside. Christmas is such a beautiful season. Life was good then. Love, protection and compassion abounded.

In my worst nightmares I never envisioned a Christmas like the year Pop was killed. Two days after, three days before his birthday. Christmas changed for me then, and try as I might I've never enjoyed another one since.

Push that memory out, forget it. Too many good ones. I guess appreciation comes from hardship and sympathy comes from pain because I appreciate what I had and feel for those who are or were denied it.

I think I'll go up and light a candle in memory of Mom and Pop.

As I walk up the aisle and kneel in front of the side altar, the Blessed Virgin Mary's altar, I can look over to the sacristy, the altar boy's side. Many a cold morning I entered church that way. The ritual is still fresh in my mind. Put on the cassock, then the surplice. The white tunic over the black garment. Next, go through the hall at the back of the altar to the priest's side, slide out the side door, over to the rectory to get the wine and water on the server's table. Next, light the candles. Lighting the candles was a fine art, one that I was really good at. After the candles were lit, it was back to the priest's side, turn the lights on in the church and then help the priest get vested for Mass. This ritual never changed.

Very few words were ever exchanged between priest and altar boys. First, it was much too early to trade pleasantries. Second, what's there to talk about between an adult man and a young boy? I can't think of a thing to say at that early hour even now, at least not without coffee. Neither coffee nor any other beverage was allowed before you received communion back then.

The ritual of Mass was the same. After you've done it so many times, you don't even think about what you have to do, you just do it. After Mass the process was reversed; the only real change occurred the day I found out what altar wine tasted like.

I had long wondered what the fruit of the vine tasted like so one day I decided to take a nip after Mass. That morning I arrived earlier than usual. I filled the cruet to the very top then headed back to church. After Mass, I lingered longer than usual. When Father Jeffers left, I headed back to the rectory with the leftover water and wine. Halfway between the priest's and altar boy's sacristies, I took my first nip of alcohol. It was my last for a very long time. Not only did it taste horrible, it burned my mouth, my throat and my stomach. I almost got sick and that was from just one little swallow. I realized why my mom and pop never drank. How could Pleasant Dale have so many bars? People must really be sick to drink all that stuff. Funny, because all the drunks seemed to be having such a great time, laughing and carrying on. It puzzled me for the longest time.

Another ritual that occurred every day happened upon arriving home. Mom asked, "What did Father say?" "Ma, he didn't say anything." "Jeri, he had to say something." "Ma, he didn't say anything." Mom believed we carried on some kind of extended conversation when the most that was ever said was, "Good morning, Father." "Good morning, Jeri." That was it.

The church was a focal point for almost everyone in the parish. Mass was almost a daily ritual for a good many people. Novenas were held every Monday night at 7:00 P.M. and during Lent, Stations of the Cross every Friday night at 7:00 P.M. Once a year we had forty hours. The church was open day and night and the devotion culminated in a festive service held at night and attended by a large portion of the priests from the diocese. Every summer the great pilgrimage to Saint Anne's Monastery in Scranton drew thousands and thousands of people. Some walked from as far away as Wilkes-Barre.

Even today, wherever I attend Mass, whether in California, Wyoming or Pennsylvania, the services and the people share a common background. The Mass has changed but the ritual has not.

One thing has changed. Now there is no one in church. As a kid I can remember people coming and going at all hours of the day, stopping by, praying silently, lighting candles or just taking a silent time to allow themselves to recoup. I don't do it much myself anymore. Maybe I should, maybe it might help put things in perspective. Not too long ago I sat with some people I work with and said a rosary. The rosary, the Hail Mary's, the Our Father's, the mysteries of the rosary, repeated over and over gave me such a relaxed feeling.

As a kid, our families gathered every night in October and May and said the rosary after supper, one of us taking turns leading every night. I can still see Mom and Pop on their knees thanking God for all we had. Pop, his hands rough, callused and twisted, coal dust so deeply imbedded in his skin that no amount of sand soap or lava could ever remove it. Mom, tired after a long day of cooking, washing and taking care of her mother and the kids. My brothers, before they went into the Air Force, my sisters Anne and Mary Kay. Our family, just a mirror of so many other families at that time, strongly bound together.

So much has changed since then. Now it's easier to eat in front of the TV and go to church only once in a while. Easier not to do than do. Like so many other things in society, if it's too hard, don't do it or let someone else do it. It's not just religion, or family; it's every phase of life.

Now, Jeri, stop it. You're preaching to yourself again. Besides, it's too hard to think about these things, let someone else do it.

Better get a move on, Jeri. Looking around, I notice the light filtering through the stained glass windows. The three aisles, the pews. Days and nights, years and decades flash through my mind like lightning on a hot summer night. How many were baptized, confirmed, married and had their own kids baptized here? How many were carried up the main aisle as a child, walked up as an adult, were wheeled up in a casket? Lives, coming and going, moving as the dust in the air moves through the filtered light of the church. Dipping my fingers in the holy water font, turning and genuflecting before the altar, I exit Saint Marie's, maybe for the last time.

⧗

My eyes blink in the sunlight. I sneeze as I always have since I was a kid whenever I moved from darkness to bright light. My mind feels clear and clean. Stopping at the church had the effect of a long cool drink of water when you're really thirsty. It was more refreshing than a glass of beer after a hard day at work.

Winter Street runs parallel to the side of the church. Taking a left on Winter Street, I walked to what we called Hemmings Hill. The hill has been paved. It was not paved when I was young. Hemmings Hill was named because the Hemming family home was located at the bottom. The hill was a favorite sledding spot for us and all the other kids in the area. A neutral spot shared by the Irish, Polish and all other nationalities. Many an hour in winter was spent careening wildly down the embankment. The hill itself was made up of a long down slope, followed by a series of smaller and smaller declines. With a good fast downward start and an uninterrupted ride, we could sometimes make it to the very top of another hill, one that led into the Polish section of the neighborhood. However, uninterrupted rides were few and far between.

The girls usually never got up enough speed to make it all the way. The boys could but also had a custom known as ditching. The hill had a ditch on either side. The object of ditching was to force another sledder into the ditches. It was fun if you did the ditching but not so much fun if you got ditched. None of us ever really got mad at being ditched. After all, you ditched, you got ditched.

Well, one day we were sleighing up a storm so to speak. I was on my way down the hill. Below me to my right, Mrs. Saluki was walking in the ditch. She was carrying two very large bags of groceries in her arms. I had a good run going, a long one. I could feel it. I remember glancing briefly to my left. Skipper Hemming had a perfect angle on me. Knowing we were going to be ditched was no big deal. We would relax and accept the inevitable, knowing there was not a whole lot we could do about it. Just then that well-known light bulb flashed in my mind. Geez, I was right in line with Mrs. Saluki. My "Oh shit" was instantly followed by a pair of legs flying over my prone body; groceries sailed all over the place. I recall Mrs. Saluki's reaction. She just lay there, skirt up over her head. Stunned and unable to move, I just stared at her. Words like "I'm sorry," tumbled out of my mouth. I was really sorry. "It's not my fault, Mrs. Saluki; Skipper ditched me."

Mrs. Saluki was on her feet and she was pissed. I'll tell you what, she really swung a mean purse. She must have hit me six or eight times. I couldn't understand a word she was saying. She was screaming at me in Polish. Her face was beet red. The more she hit me, the more she seemed to want to hit me. I wanted her to hit me. Harder, Mrs. Saluki, and when you're finished go after Skipper Hemming; he caused it. But no, I got the brunt of it. She spent her fury on me. I never felt a thing. Before we were allowed to go sledding we were bundled up, and I mean bundled up. It took twenty minutes to get dressed. I could have been hit by a truck and not felt a thing. Mrs. Saluki lapsed back into English, "Wait till I tell your mother." Oh no. "Mrs. Saluki, please. I didn't mean it." She must have been rested up because she hit me again. I kept thinking, "Hit me some more, but don't tell my mom." She lapsed back into Polish. I got my wish. She hit me some more. Back to English. "Docerty, you help me pick up these groceries." "Yes, Mrs. Saluki, please don't tell my mom." "Help me pick up these groceries you little _____." I couldn't understand the last word; it must have been Polish. I put the groceries on my sled and took them to her house. She never let up on me; she must have called me every Polish curse word in the books.

On my way back up the hill, I thought of running away from home, but I knew that was hopeless. First, it was too cold; second, Mom would find me, then I'd really be in a lot more trouble than I was already. Why didn't I get killed? I could have been hit by a car and been on my way to purgatory by now. I went home, but Mom didn't say a thing.

"Maybe she's just waiting for Pop to get home," I thought. Now Mom never waited; she just made sure I waited till "Pop got home." I wanted to thank Mrs. Saluki; she never told Mom. I tried to thank her once a few weeks later but she just yelled something in Polish at me. I guess I was not her favorite person.

Not all my sledding adventures turned out as well. We had two sleds in our family. One was the girls'. The girls' sled did not go very fast; it did, however, steer. The boys' sled on the other hand went very fast but the steering mechanism didn't work. To steer you had to shift your body weight right or left and needless to say, there was no braking system. On the particular day in question, I was making my umpteenth trip down the hill, flying like the wind, when the worst possible thing happened. I lost control. A car parked in front of a house at the bottom of the hill and I became best friends. The only part of me susceptible to injury was my head and that's exactly where I met the car. Its bumper and my forehead joined. I stopped dead; the sled kept going. It had to be hilarious to watch, but not from my vantage point. That shiny chrome bumper, I probably could see my reflection in it. I might have been able to smile at myself.

I didn't get knocked out, I don't think. My football coaches used to call it getting your bell rung. My bell rang and rang. I had visions of stars flashing before my eyes. I saw stars, but not only stars. I saw moons, planets, the universe, the cosmos. My brother was delivering groceries for Fallon's Store at the time. He saw the whole thing. He came over and put me on the sleigh. Funny, there were two of him. Come to think of it there were two Jim McAndrews, two Joe Gradys, two Sean Doyles, two cars. I closed one eye. Great, there's only one and a half of everybody. My forehead hurt like heck. My brother Don put the grocery box he was carrying over my head. The bells were echoing off the sides of the box. I wasn't seeing two of everything anymore, just cardboard.

I vaguely remember Don warning me not to tell Mom. He must think I'm an idiot. "Tell Mom? Are you nuts?" I mumbled. "What?" he replied. "What?" I questioned. "Shut up, Jeri." "What?" "Shut up, you idiot." "Yeah, okay Don." Tell Mom; he must be crazy. She'd kill me; then she'd kill him. Now even though Don had nothing to do with my hitting that car, Mom would have tied him into it somehow. "You should have been watching him." Then Don, unable to help himself would have said something smart like, "I was watching him. I think he moved the car back a foot or two." Now Mom would really be mad. No. Me tell Mom, never.

He got me home, my ears still ringing, but at least there was only a little more than one of him now. He helped me pull off my snowsuit. No easy feat. He sat me in front of the TV and turned on one of the soap operas for kids, *The Atomic Man*. I'm not sure whether reception was bad or a snowstorm was in progress in my head. *The Atomic Man* was very, very short and awfully wide. It reminds me now of watching a 3D movie without the glasses.

Mom never suspected a thing. I guess I appeared no more dazed than I usually did. The red mark across my forehead, like my rosy cheeks, was probably attributed to the cold weather. The headache lasted a week. I suffered in silence, living by the unspoken motto, "Never let them know you're hurt."

There were other hills in town, steeper hills, closed off for us kids. They were all above Main Street, hills like

School Street and McAlpine Street. No cars used them in the winter, just kids on sleds. They were long runs that ended a block before Main Street. The whole block was covered with coal ashes to insure no little ones traveled the length of that block to Main Street and traffic. They, the adults, took care of us. They knew where we were because they joined us.

Of all the streets opened for sledding, our favorite was Hemmy's Hill. Local, less crowded like a sparsely used ski run, you got more runs for energy. Looking down the now-paved street, memories of cold afternoons and evenings arise. Cold air burning our lungs. Lumps of snow frozen to our snowsuits. Like little Michelin tire figures we'd spend our winters. Yeah, Jeri, winters of our content.

⧗

Turning back towards Blackthorne Street, I see the concrete curbing. As a teen, I dug the ditches to put that curbing in. It's not new and squared anymore but then again, Jeri, you're not as squared and fresh anymore either. Sobering thought.

Less than a block away is 811 Blackthorne Street. I remember the last time I was in the house. Throwing away all the unwanted articles. Loading them in the pickup truck. Taking them to the town dump. A sad task. Old bed frames and discarded articles of clothing. A last look around. Then turning the key over to Tom Gibson, the new owner. A lifetime ago.

I'm drawn to the house like a magnet. Still the pull is a slow one. I'm not sure what I'll see. What memories will arise, if any? As a little kid, I helped paint the house, much to the dismay of my mom and pop. I don't remember the incident. My brothers and my sister Anne, however, described it to me. Onney McAndrews was hired to paint the house white with green trim. I was very young and in the way. Onney gave me a brush. No paint, just a brush. I was painting without paint. Well, after Onney left, I found some paint, red enamel paint. I then proceeded to paint a red stripe around the house. Needless to say it was very low to the ground. No one noticed me or my work. That is, no one noticed until Pop got home. Boy, did he notice. (I'm also told I once tried to paint one of the cats in the neighborhood but I failed. The cat was a lot swifter than I.) Pop was mad, but nothing was done to me. After all my intentions were good and industrious. You don't punish a kid for showing good work habits. It must have been tough to paint over red enamel with flat white paint.

Turning left on Blackthorne Street, St. Marie's Convent looms in front of me. It's just as big and imposing as it was when I was a kid. The dark red brick, three stories high, with an enormous concrete flooded basement. I remember that basement well. I spent enough time down there mixing Sister Julia's fertilizer for her flower garden. Sister was a tremendous gardener. Her flowers adorned the altars of the church and the convent. If odor of a fertilizer is any indication of power to enhance growth, it's a wonder her roses weren't the size of pine trees. She used three or four different kinds of liquids that had to be mixed in the right proportions. The smell was enough to gag a maggot. Gag me, it did. But Sister was such a good soul, I never really minded helping her.

Another plus in helping her was a little booster in grades plus a good word to Mom. "What a good boy he is, Mrs. Docerty." Of course I never heard her say anything bad about anyone, but that "He's such a good boy" always gave Mom reason to hope about my eventual outcome.

Sister Julia was not the only nun we helped. Mom was into helping everyone. "Jeri, go over and help shovel the snow off the sidewalks in front of the convent." "Yes, Mom." There was never any argument about helping. Never any "How much am I going to get for it?" You just did it. I helped shovel not only the convent's sidewalk, but sometimes the entire block down to Winter Street. "Jeri, help Mrs. White, and poor Mrs. Keesey. Mr. Keesey's sick. Shovel her sidewalk, too." Now there was only one more house left on the street. "Jeri, give Mr. McDermitt a hand. I'm sure he'd appreciate it." By then I'd have covered the entire block, both sides. Mom firmly believed that a tired boy was a healthy boy.

Looking up the block, I can see exactly why I hate to shovel snow even now. It never hurt me. The kids in the area often did a lot to help the older people in the neighborhood. Run for groceries, cut grass, help shovel snow, carry out ashes, and we did it all without asking, "How much do we get?" Things would seem to work out for us in Christmas presents, cookies, candy and any number of niceties. Ask a kid now to do something for you and the first thing out of their mouth is, "What do I get for it?"

Looking up at the convent, I can visualize the interior. As a kid, it always seemed cold, sterile and somber. We were never tempted to laugh when we were in its hallowed halls. It surely had to be some kind of sin. Periodically, we'd help scrub floors, polish furniture and other such tasks.

That place was so clean you could eat off the floor; so quiet you could hear a pin drop.

One of my worst fears was to be called over to the convent for a conference. I would feel my stomach turn at the prospect. Mom, Sister and me. Never a good outcome. Two against one. No fair.

Serving Mass there, usually when my uncle, Father Nilus, was visiting, was an early morning event. It seemed the nuns got up way before the sun rose. I can't recall the exact time, but it was dark, not only before Mass but even after Mass. I remember walking down the halls, expecting a nun to step out of one of the rooms in her PJs. I always thought their pajamas were a lot like their habits, black and white starched material. I never found out. The nuns were always sitting in the chapel singing some kind of Latin song or praying one of their litanies. I always figured they were up for hours waiting for us. Walking down the halls, the sounds of my shoes hitting the polished floors echoed like cannon shots across a valley. Amazingly, the nuns walked silently, they could walk up right behind you and scare the bejesus out of you. They glided noiselessly across solid surfaces. The only time we'd know they were there was when we'd receive a swat across the back of the head for some offense. School, church or outdoors, they zeroed in on offending kids like laser-controlled aircraft. Whack, I got you! They must have learned these skills in the novitiate. Silent stalking 101 and 102, later stalking on a graduate level, 501 and 502.

The chapel in the convent was a miniature version of the church. Those morning chapel Masses gave me a glimpse of the life of a nun during that time period. Austere, communal, very few outside pleasures. I admired the dedication and devotion of these women. They spent their lives in prayer and service. It had to be a tremendous sacrifice. Of course, at the time, I was scared to death of them. Their word was gospel. They were a law unto themselves. The dreaded words, usually uttered from a mother holding a phone, "He did what?" paralyzed us. Still it was their constant harping that helped educate us, taught us discipline and respect.

⧗

Looking away from the convent I can see the house— 811 Blackthorne Street.

The house seems different, remodeled. The hedges gone; trees trimmed back. Reluctantly, I approach our side of the duplex. I feel strangely disjoined. No longer myself, but a shy little red-haired kid, covered with freckles. Passing images swim by. Images of Jim, Spike, Sean, Joe and me headed uptown. Up to Lenny Leed's to cash in some soda bottles and get some candy. We glance over to the alley in back of the convent. Our pace quickens; we cross the street. Then the sudden rush of adrenaline. "Race ya there." The challenge issued, that gauntlet thrown, we run. Arms pumping furiously, hands clutching our prized bottles, our feet speed across the ground, sure of ourselves, our goal. We jostle for position, holding back for the final sprint up the alley between the movie theater and Murray's store. The pack thins as we break out onto Main Street. Lenny's now only a mere fifteen yards away. Time to kick in the afterburners. Our race ends as we speed past Lenny's, unable to slow down in time. Gasping, laughing, slapping each other on the backs and arms. Buddies not really caring who won, like young sleek dogs chasing imaginary game across a field, our run of life. We are alive, we have collateral and we would soon have candy. Yeah, it doesn't get any better than this. The image fades as quickly as it appeared.

How many times did we run that alley? How many "Race ya there's" were yelled? How many years have passed since I really enjoyed a race to anywhere? Now, it's race to work, race home, run here, run there, traffic, time schedules, idiot drivers, traffic jams. Now getting there is not fun, not an adventure; it's a job. It's frustration. Enough, Jeri. The run of life, the rush of youth, that was fun. The seeming madness of maturity, that's not.

Glancing back at the house, looking up at the porch, visions of Mom and Pop awaken. I see them sitting there on a warm June evening, not saying much, just checking out the neighborhood. Thinking of Pop sitting there. Hearing him say, "Guy, if I had a million dollars, I'd just sit here and watch the world go by." From time to time, Pop called me Guy, his nickname for me. Mom, rocking back and forth, I'm sure she felt as he did. Just sit there and watch the world go by. They never got that chance.

It seems so unfair. I've seen and known all kinds of people in my life. Some aren't worth the space they occupy, yet they seem to be the ones who suffer the least. People who have every material comfort receive all the advantages and work the least for what they have. They want and get more and still that's not enough for them. All that Mom and Pop wanted was to see their kids grow up to be decent people, to play with their grandchildren and to grow old gracefully together, but they didn't get the chance. They died young. Maybe that's why we all worked so hard to achieve, contribute, to be good and decent people. I know that's what drove and still drives me.

The porch. God, I remember when they put the new flooring on it. I was a little kid with nothing to do except bug the carpenter. I guess the same as I did the painter, except I was a little older, because I remember that day. "Let me help you. Let me help you." "Ok, Jeri, sit on the board and steady it while I saw it." Yeah, doing man's work and only five years old! It got boring just sitting there. Wait, I'll bet I can really help him by brushing the sawdust away from the saw. "Holy shit, Jeri, what the hell?" Then the more serious, "Jesus, Mary and Joseph." I never felt a thing, maybe a little pinch, but no pain. What was he so excited about? "Jesus, Mary and Joseph and all the saints." "Doc, I think I sawed the kid's finger off."

Doc, my father, was there in a flash. What's everybody so excited about? Then my hand felt strange. I looked down. Oh-oh! my hand was covered with blood. Pop picked me up and ran around back and into the kitchen. Mom saw me. "Oh my God, Donald, what happened?" "He stuck his hand under the saw." Mom's gone bananas by now. "Jesus, Mary and Joseph. Francis, get over here and hold your brother's little finger." What's everybody so excited about? Pop picks me up; I'm bleeding like a stuck pig. Francis, my brother, is holding onto my finger, which is hanging by a thread, they walk out carefully to the pickup truck, the carpenter is saying something about being sorry. I look at him; he almost looks as if he's crying. "I didn't mean it, Doc." "I know; it's not your fault."

We're in the truck. Now I'm scared. I'm bleeding into Pop's toolbox, which is on the seat. I keep thinking he's going to be mad at me. I know how sticky blood gets and his tools are really going to be sticky, that's for sure. "Guy, if you don't cry, I'll take you to the movies tonight." No problem. See the pain didn't kick in yet. "Don't let go of his finger, Frannie." "I won't, Pop."

My brother Fran told me years later that my finger was just hanging there and he had this terrible urge to just give it a yank. But loving brother that he was, he resisted the urge. We got to old Doc Duffy's office in record time. I guess the Doc was so used to patching up miners he just sewed the thing back on the hand. He told Pop something but I don't know what. I had this huge bandage on my hand when I left his office. I remember the ride home. Pop talking to me. My brother Francis close to me, all seemed great. I got to go to the movies that night and Pop took me. Not a bad deal considering. Mom gave me a big hug when I got home. My poor sister Anne. Mom lit into her. "You should have been watching him." Et cetera, et cetera. Poor Anne wasn't even home. She was down at church helping decorate the altar with Sister Julia's flowers. I guess Mom had to blow off steam and she wasn't going to yell at me because I was young and stupid, but she should have. After all, it was my fault.

Mom fixed me something special that night for supper and Pop, true to his word, took me to the movies.

The human body is a rather funny piece of equipment, especially the pain part. The finger didn't hurt me until that night; at the movies is when the pain kicked in. One thought kept running through my head. Jesus, Mary and Joseph, does my hand hurt. I can't remember the name of the movie. I was in pain. Pop, however, got interested in the show. I wanted to go home, but Pop kept saying, "In a minute," which I knew meant we were watching the whole thing. Well, the finger healed, but I have never really ever been able to straighten it out fully. That's life, Jeri.

⌛

Pop fixed the porch in sections, first the flooring. Then, I guess he'd save some money and do the sides. The railing that went around the front of the house was closed in by using wood shingles on the outside and some kind of wood paneling on the inside. When they were fixing the railing, the old discarded pieces of wood and nails were thrown in the front yard to be cleaned up after the job was completed. Pop did most of the work on his time off from work so it was slow going.

One day, a summer afternoon, a bunch of us were playing paratrooper. The game was easy. We stood on the railing, yelled "Geronimo" and jumped. We had to jump out far enough to clear the small sidewalk that went around the house to the back porch. It was not a very far leap. Leap, "Geronimo," hit the grass, get up, run up the steps and do it again. Like most of our games, we played until we were exhausted or bored, whichever came first. Bart Barry was playing with us on this particular day.

Bart never really became part of our group. He left the neighborhood and they tore down his house, but Bart was there that day. I never liked Bart all that much. He was kind of a bully, but he played with us on occasion. Well, Bart leaped into space, pulled his imaginary rip cord, yelled "Geronimo," hit the ground, rolled and came up screaming. When Bart rolled, he got a nail stuck in his head. Not much damage but a lot of blood. We would have awarded him the Purple Heart, but he ran home crying. Ah, war wounds. Mom heard the commotion, came out and after a few choice words about being the death of her, we were forbidden to bail out over my front yard anymore. Too bad because it was the best spot in the neighborhood for skydiving. Other porches were either too high, too low or just too dangerous, and when we considered something too dangerous, it probably would have killed one of us.

Another thing I remember about the porch was heavy snowstorms. Mom would tie a rope around my waist and I would get out on the roof and shovel the snow off to keep the roof from collapsing. I convinced Mom that it would be best if she tied me to the radiator because if I slipped the only thing the rope would do would pull her down on top of me. I had visions of both of us heading down a snowy roof, kind of ski jumping into eternity. I can still see her in the window, "Be careful, Jeri." "Yeah Ma." The rope was tied to the radiator but Mom still held on to it.

⧖

There was a group of men in town we called "the bottle gang." These guys were down-and-out alcoholics. They'd chip in and buy a few bottles of cheap wine or whiskey and then go find some field where they'd sit and get drunk. I didn't know any of them by name. These were men whose lives slipped out of control. They'd drink their problems away until their forgotten troubles were replaced with a more serious one: alcoholism.

Mom and I were sitting on the front porch late one Saturday afternoon watching people on their way to confession. Mom saw one of these men sneak down the alley and hide a bottle at the back of Holahan's garage. When he left, she told me to go get it, which I did. Mom was bent on teaching this man a lesson, so she took the bottle, marked the level of the contents then poured it down the kitchen sink. She made tea to about the consistency of the color of the whiskey and then refilled the bottle to its original level. I was instructed to put it back where I found it. Mom had a sense of humor. We never did see the man retrieve it, but it was gone the next morning. I wonder what the man thought when he took the first healthy pull on the bottle of Four Roses. Miracle of the wedding feast at Cana in reverse. Whiskey into tea, a sign from above. Chalk one up for Mom.

The alley that separated our property from the Fallons seems to have disappeared over the years. Probably better for me not to venture that way. The alley served as a short-cut to the bakery and Kristenson's Grocery Store. The grocery store sold Polish hams and meats. The people who owned it were Polish. Their name was probably changed, like so many immigrants' names, by immigration officials who either couldn't spell the name or were too lazy to spell it correctly. Americanized.

Mom used to send us on different errands. She always wrote notes for me. Mom didn't trust my memory. One day in particular, Mom sent me to the bakery for a dozen assorted rolls. "Let me write it out for you, Jeri." "No, Ma, I can remember." "You'd better." "Ma, I'll remember." Off I went. I'll show her I can remember, dazzle her with my keen mind. All the way up the alley I kept repeating, over and over, a dozen assorted, a dozen assorted. Piece of cake, no problem, got it made. A dozen assorted, a dozen assorted. Like the Greek messenger delivering the news of victory on the plains of Marathon, I flew like the wind. A dozen assorted, a dozen assorted. Turning right at the bottom of the alley, I made my way up the narrow passageway between the houses onto Main Street. A dozen assorted. I'll impress the ladies at the bakery with my memory. A dozen assorted. Slow down, catch your breath. A dozen assorted. Now through the front door of the bakery. A dozen assorted. Finally my turn came. "What do you want, Jeri?" "A dozen assorted." "A dozen assorted what?" Ah, no fair. "A dozen assorted cupcakes, donuts, cookies, rolls, what?" She had me there. All I remembered was "a dozen assorted." "Can I use your phone?" "Yes, Jeri." "Hello Mom, a dozen assorted what?" "Rolls, Jeri, rolls." "Oh, yeah." I got the dozen assorted rolls and headed back home the long, slow way. Mom would not be trusting me for some time.

My sister, Anne, told me at one of our reunions that Mom put the phone down after that call, shook her head and said, "I don't know what I'm going to do with that boy." Of course, the ladies at the bakery weren't any help. After that incident, they would play it over in full. The scene would always go something like this: "I want six cupcakes, six chocolate chip cookies and a half dozen poppy seed rolls." "Are you sure, Jeri?" "Uh, can I use your phone?" Just that little shade of doubt in their voices was enough to trigger that little voice in my mind. "No, I'm not sure, at least not anymore." I must have been good for a lot of laughs at the bakery.

⧗

I must look odd standing here staring at the house. The house is just that, a house. It's not the home I remember. It's someone else's home now. I'm tempted to go to the front door, knock and ask if I can look around. I know better.

I think I'll take a walk up to May's Bar and have a beer. It'll be nice to sit for a few minutes. I guess I can remember there as well as here. May's is just a block away. Mom and Pop didn't drink. I can remember someone telling me one time that there were only two kinds of Irish. The ones who didn't drink and the ones who tried to make up for it by drinking twice as much to take up the slack for the temperate ones.

Once I was helping Pop clean out an old mine in Laffland, a small mining town that was mostly deserted. It was the kind of town with old barracks-like buildings that served as homes for miners. Company homes they were called. Dirt streets. In the center of this little community was a store. I gathered it had been the company store at one time. Pop and I took a break around noon. We walked over to the store to buy some lunchmeat and bread for sandwiches. The guy who ran the store asked Pop if he wanted a beer; Pop said, "No." He then asked if the boy, me, wanted one. I was about twelve years old at the time. It was not an uncommon thing for some families, because of their culture, to allow their kids a beer or wine. Not ours. My Dad's reply still sticks in my mind. "If I ever catch the boy with a beer in his hand, I'll break the bottle over his head." Nothing like a little subtlety. I did, however, get the message. Pop did not like drinking. There had to be a reason he detested it so much, but I never found out why. My brothers and sisters surmised that Pop's dad was an alcoholic, but we never knew for sure. Relatives raised Pop and my Aunt Jerri; he never spoke of his father.

My sister Anne told me one time about Mom being at a wedding. Anne told her the punch was nonalcoholic so Mom drank a few. The more she had, the funnier she got. When they got home, Mom fell asleep on the couch where she remained until the following morning. Mom woke up with a bad case of the flu. Headache, upset stomach, it must have been the flu. Of course, no one ever told her of probably the only drinking spree she ever unknowingly engaged in.

⧗

Trudging up the hill toward Main Street brings to mind the three years I spent as a safety patrol boy. Starting in sixth grade I received the prized white belt with the silver badge, my symbol of office, a duty not lightly delegated by the IHM nuns who ran our school. Over the next three years, I worked my way up to safety patrol captain. Needless to say, I took my job seriously. Young lives hung in the balance. With our credo, "Safety first," etched into our minds, we'd maneuver our charges like small herds of human cattle across the intersections.

At Winter Street, our charges split. One group headed up Blackthorne on the right hand side while my group made their way up the left, past my house, across the alley up to Main Street. "Close it up back there; slow down up there; the little ones can't keep up." Ah, yes. Head 'em up, move 'em out. Once up to Main Street, we'd hold the group until the traffic light turned green. Then, without regard for personal safety, we patrol boys stepped into the street, raised our hands with palms facing towards traffic while our charges crossed the intersection and made their way safely to their individual homes.

One day while performing my duty, I happened to look down Blackthorne Street and notice some stragglers. I motioned to them to get a move on. However, they did not seem to hasten their pace. I'd have to give them a good old-fashioned tongue lashing for their tardiness. The traffic light turned green which meant traffic should be allowed to move freely on Main Street, but I stood my post unmoved by the color of a mere traffic light. After all, my charges needed crossing. I waited patiently despite the man in the car blowing his horn and shaking his fist at me. The kids finally got to the intersection, but they did not cross. Instead, they entered Fallon's Store. I was embarrassed but I couldn't show any emotion. After all, I was a professional. With all the confidence I could muster, I simply turned toward each direction and motioned traffic forward. The man in the car facing me, the man who was yelling and blowing the horn, turned towards me as he drove past and shot me the finger. He shot me the bird just for doing my duty. Such a thankless job.

As I turned to head home, it dawned on me that I was wrong in what I had done. We had always been told, "Never, ever cross against the light." What if that man called the nuns and told on me? Pictures of my being drummed from the corps in disgrace, my precious captain's badge being torn from my bleached white safety patrol belt arose in my imagination. My walk broke into a run. For the next few days, I waited to be called into the Mother Superior's presence to face what would amount to the grade school equivalent of a court-martial. I lucked out. No charges were ever pressed and I served out my captaincy without further incident.

☒

Another trip down memory lane carried me the length of the hill to the traffic light without my being aware that I was even walking. The old traffic lights, those four metal posts, one placed on each corner, have since been replaced by a more modern wire suspension traffic signal. Turning left, moving up Main Street toward May's Bar, I passed what used to be Fallon's Store. The Fallons' house is a large three-story structure that has been remodeled, like a lot of homes in the area. It is right next to the store. I know that the house was converted into apartments years ago; I lived for a time in the one in the attic. I can see the one window on the first floor in front, the one that was located where the parlor was. Back then there was always one room in every house that was off limits to children, that was the parlor.

I remember our parlor with its brand new furniture. The few times it was ever used were for funerals; the body of the deceased waked there. The other times were reserved for special company. Our parlor contained a piano; we could go in and play chopsticks on it but we best not sit on the chairs or sofa. Like all forbidden places, it offered a challenge to kids. Spike Fallon and I sneaked into their parlor one evening. His father was working at the store and his mom was out somewhere. We were jumping from the arm of the sofa onto the very new, very springy cushions. Somersaults, flips, belly floppers. We were having a good old time until . . .

Mrs. Fallon had these two "priceless" lamps dating back to the Ming Dynasty. Now I could never figure out why people would pay so much for stupid lamps, but according to her they were worth fifty dollars. It was my turn; I did a high half-gainer, bounced too high and caught the edge of the lamp with my heel, the rest of the sequence of action took place in slow motion, much like a modern slow moving videotape of Michael Jordan doing one of his flying, leaping slam dunks. The lamp teetered back and forth. Then slowly, every so slowly, it took a downward tumble towards the floor and destruction. Now as quick as both Spike and I were, even a leaping dive would be too little, too late. The lamp hit and broke into about a dozen pieces, far too many to glue back together unnoticed. Very little phased Spike, but he knew and I knew we were now in major difficulty.

I excused myself, much to Spike's dismay and beat a hasty retreat home, hoping against hope that lamp would suddenly, like the legendary Phoenix, rise from the ashes out of destruction. It didn't happen. When Mom found out, it was another, "Wait till your father gets home" day. Pop was not pleased. Fifty bucks was a far cry from a second creamsicle. I never found out how the debt was settled, or if it ever was. It was probably chalked up to an act of God.

One day I was on my way to Louie the barber to get a haircut when Spike saw me and asked if he could go along. "Sure, Spike." We were walking towards Louie's when Spike spotted his cousin, Jimmie Linden. Spike and Jimmie hated each other. Jimmy lived in Mousic, the next town to Pleasant Dale if you were going towards Scranton. Jimmie usually took off when he saw Spike mainly because Spike used to beat him up every time they met. So much for blood being thicker than water, although blood would be an appropriate word to connect with their relationship. I never asked Spike why he hated Jimmie. I just figured it was none of my business.

On this particular day, Jimmie did not turn and run. This surprised me but seemed to delight Spike. Like two movie gunfighters, their pace slowed. They drew nearer each other. I remember Jim had his right hand behind his back. Like the movie bystander, I moved off to the side. They were now face to face exchanging what I didn't consider pleasantries. Quick as a flash Jimmie's hand came from behind his back revealing a piece of lath board. Lath board was a piece of rough wood that was used as a base for plastering before the introduction of dry wall. We often used these pieces of wood to make swords, which explains why we were always digging splinters out of our fingers and hands. Jimmie took a stand, tired of getting beat up. He struck Spike with his sword of retribution. What he failed to consider in this act of vengeance was the results of this action.

The board hit Spike flush in the left side of his face driving a three-inch splinter completely through Spike's upper lip. Blood spurted out. Jimmie dropped his weapon, turned and made tracks toward Mousic. Spike screamed in pain. I stood dumbfounded. Spike looked like a human walrus with one tusk intact and the other missing.

Spike made for his house leaving a trail of blood behind him. I ran to the store and got Mr. Fallon. Together we followed Spike's blood trail, which led into the house and down the hall to Spike's bedroom, but Spike was nowhere in sight. There was a large splotch of blood below the bed. Mr. Fallon looked underneath and spotted Spike. Spike threw a shoe at him. He reached under the bed to grab Spike. Spike hit his father's hand with the other shoe. It was a standoff. Mr. Fallon tried to talk Spike out from underneath the bed. Spike refused. In the meantime, Spike's mom called Dr. Duffy who got there in ten minutes. Neither Mr. nor Mrs. Fallon could get Spike out. My words trying to coax Spike out fell on deaf ears. Spike could not be budged. Doc Duffy tried to tell Spike he'd feel a whole lot better if he'd let him pull that sliver out of his lip. Spike was satisfied with his new look. Finally, Mr. Fallon sent for my brother, Don. A good move.

Spike and Don had a real working relationship. A few months before Spike had hit Don in the face with a shovel and chipped his front tooth. Don then proceeded to beat Spike to within an inch of his life, all the while telling Spike what would happen to him if he were ever foolish enough to try to repeat such behavior. Spike respected Don as Spike seemed to respect few others. Don arrived, lay down on the floor next to the bed and told Spike what would happen if he hit him with the shoe. Don then grabbed Spike's arm, pulled him out, stood him up and held his arms while Doc Duffy pulled the splinter out. All this happened so quickly that Spike didn't feel a thing. Spike did not look all that well for the next few days, but he no longer looked like a one-tusked walrus.

⧖

Main Street. All these houses and the street seem vaguely familiar. They are not as I remember them, but when I look at where Spike lived it comes back to me as though it were yesterday. If I lived here day in and day out,

I'd pass these places much as I pass places in York, ignoring all but the center of focus, whether it's driving home or to the store or stopping for a beer. I'm sure it would be the same if I lived here. It's funny how much I actually left behind in the relatively short span of time I was here. I wonder if Jim, Sean, Joe or any of the other guys who might have stayed here, pass these places without a thought of their past.

May's is just down the street, a little past where Louie the barber's used to be. Louie's was the place for the bimonthly haircut; there was a seat that was attached to the arm of the chair to accommodate the smaller of us customers. Eventually, we'd sit on the chair's actual seat, a sign of growth. Our haircut would be accompanied by the straight razor that was used to accent the side burns and back of the neck. Ah, another step closer to shaving.

May's used to be owned by a Polish couple that I remember because of their son. Their son played the accordion and played it very badly. I remember being down around the Hemmings' backyard at night listening to him practice. It sent chills through me; he was terrible. The accordion is one of the main instruments in a Polish band. These bands played at weddings, parties and all the other festive occasions in the coal regions. I don't care what nationality was getting married: Irish, Polish, Russian or Italian. All the bands had an accordion player. Polka music. Ah yes. And a one and a two. We'd Pennsylvania, Beer Barrel or Whatever Polka our way through receptions and block parties. It was easy to dance to and fun to listen to. Polkas were light, lively and energetic, except when you heard this kid play them.

May's bar is only one of many bars that dotted this town and many others of the region. One evening a bunch of us sat down and counted the number of bars and clubs in town and we came up with sixteen legal ones. There were illegal ones. It was quite a number for a town that probably had fewer than 3,500 people. Start at one end of town, drink one beer in every bar in town, you'd end up in la-la land. An illegal bar was really not set up like a bar. They were houses where men gathered to play cards. The house got a small percentage of the pot, sold beer, food, whiskey, soda, whatever.

One such illegal establishment was at the top of a large hill on Airport Street. My pop didn't drink but every Friday night he played penny ante poker at that illegal bar. Moreover, every Friday Pop would take me along with him. I really loved those nights and always looked forward to going. Pop would go down into the basement where they played cards and I'd sit upstairs and watch TV. Soda, pretzels, chips and candy were lavished on me. The men would occasionally come upstairs and give me a few pennies or a soda or whatever. It was on these nights that I got to watch the Friday night fights. The theme song and words from it still echo in my mind: "To look sharp and be on the ball, to feel sharp." Et cetera, et cetera. Gillette blue blades. I got to see some great boxing.

Pop took me as he had taken my brothers before me. In the same way he took me fishing with him on Sundays during spring and summer. I looked forward to the time when I was old enough to go fishing with Pop. We'd wake up early and go to the 6:00 A.M. Mass. When we got home from Mass, Pop would make eggs and his famous home fries. I have never been able to make home fries that tasted that good. Then we'd head over to Drury to get some live bait. Almost every Sunday we'd fish at Lake Ariel.

My first time fishing with Pop he rowed the boat, at least part of the way, out to the middle. That was the last time he rowed the boat as long as I fished with him. Pop would have made a good psychologist; he certainly understood me. "Pop, let me row." "No Guy, you're not strong enough yet." "Yes I am, Pop. Please let me row." "Well, OK, Guy, if you think you can." That was it; I rowed and rowed and rowed. I really didn't mind all that much. I still like to row boats.

I have to admit I was not much of a fisherman. Fishing with Pop was a long, long day because Pop loved to fish. We never brought a whole lot of food with us. We'd cook the fish we caught on an island at the end of the lake. Pop taught me to gut and scale fish, which also became my job upon arriving home. Pop would take a stick, put a little butter on the inside of the fish, tie it off with a wire and we'd cook it over the fire. He put a pot of water on for tea. In the pot he'd place a can of pork and beans. That was our dinner. There were times when the beans spilled over into the water. This really gave the tea an unusual taste. It was simple, it was fun and it was with Pop.

⧗

Walking into May's almost blinds me. Coming from bright sunlight to a dark narrow bar takes adjusting. There are only two people at the bar, plus the bartender. I don't recognize either of the customers or the bartender. Whenever a stranger comes into a neighborhood bar like this, people give him the once over. I'm no exception. "What'll you have?" "Give me a glass of Steg." Steg is a local beer.

It feels good to sit down. I feel kind of tired physically, but emotionally I feel great. I can see my reflection in the mirror. Not the little freckled faced red-haired kid anymore, are you, Jeri? I wonder what it would be like to spend a week here. Look up some old friends like Patty, Margie, Mary Jean and Mary if they're still around. These girls entered my life after grade school. Before that we never had time for girls. Girls seemed to be something we tolerated but never really cared for.

Then came puberty. All those hormones racing wildly through our bodies changed everything. Life took on a more serious tone. Still I remember those pre-puberty times. I look at kids that age now and I wonder if they are having the fun we had. I don't think I'd like to grow up now, far too many things available, too much organization, too much real danger. Danger from psychos, nuts, perverts. It's no wonder there is so much paranoia today. However, it's not a false fear; the fear is real. We never felt that fear as kids.

Today things seem easier. Cable TV, remote controls. Oh yeah, remote controls. I used to think they were the height of laziness. My mom used to use the expression and so did the nuns, "That, young man, is the height of laziness." I have a remote and I'd search ten minutes to find it rather than just get up to change the stupid channel. Like the song "57 Channels and Nothing On." Cable. Tooling around the channels with my remote and nothing is on, bored out of my mind. If it's too hot, turn on the air conditioner, if it's too cold turn up the heat. God, I'm spoiled.

I remember waking up in the morning during the winter, the house freezing cold. The boys' room had no heat and only one window. Mom gave you a wake up call, "Come on boys, get up, time from school." We tried to ignore her, pulling the blanket over our heads. The second call was not quite as pleasant, "Get up, you're going to be late for school." We knew we had to get up. Even if we were wide awake it was the thought of hitting the cold linoleum floor followed by the sprint downstairs to the kitchen where Mom had the oven door open for heat. My brother Don and I shared the double bed. Fran, my oldest brother, had the single bed. Being the youngest, I usually was the first one out of bed, sometimes it was not by choice. Like a sacrificial lamb offered to appease the gods, I was tossed out of bed to appease Mom.

Once out we had to move. Move or freeze, no putting on clothes, it was too cold, hit the floor and run. It was better for me that way. It seems as you get older you get grouchier, at least that was the case with my brothers, so I got out of harm's way. Once in the kitchen we'd grab a chair and sit in front of the oven with our feet stuck in the open door. Once warmed, we'd sit down and eat our oatmeal with a lot of sugar and drink coffee, also with a lot of sugar and cream in it.

In summer the breakfast fare changed to Nabisco Shredded Wheat. It was simple to make. Take two of the shredded biscuits, put them in a bowl and run hot water over them. When they were sufficiently softened, you added milk and sugar. Mom would squeeze fresh orange juice on special occasions. When summer rolled around the bedroom that lacked heat in winter became our nemesis. It would get so hot in that bedroom with only one window that I'd wake up soaking wet and gulping air like a beached fish. Mom wouldn't let us sleep out on the front porch.

"You'll scandalize the nuns." Now I always had trouble figuring the logic behind this statement. How can a sleeping boy scandalize anyone? Mom was steadfast on the issue of nuns and scandalization. Pop walked around the house with his shirt off and I can still hear Mom. "Donald, put your shirt on, do you want to scandalize the nuns?" I never said it but I always thought how in God's name could they see him in our living room unless they used a reverse periscope? We didn't argue with Mom about religion, nuns, priests or school. As a matter of fact, we didn't argue with Mom about anything. I'd sneak downstairs in summer when it got unbearably hot in the bedroom. I took my chances and somehow I never got caught.

The only real comfortable months were spring and fall when it was neither too hot nor too cold. It really didn't matter about the temperature of the house because we never spent that much time inside. Hottest or coldest days didn't matter, the moms in the area believed in outside activity.

At the time, I believed what they said about strong bodies, strong minds. Healthy glow to your face in winter, sunburn in summer—it's good for you. "The idle mind is the devil's workshop." Now as an adult and a schoolteacher, I know the real reason for all the outdoor activity. We drove them nuts when we were indoors. It was all for their benefit. By the time we came indoors we'd be exhausted and an exhausted kid is a quiet kid. They were right, of course. As we grew, we grew stronger, healthier and more inventive. Our games never ended.

Thinking back on it as I am now, I don't recall any of the kids I hung around with being unhappy. Oh, we'd have our bad days, but to my knowledge none of my friends were abused, unwanted or neglected, but they weren't pampered either. Our parents were just that—parents. They weren't our buddies or pals. We didn't call them by their first names. When we got in trouble in or out of school, we knew exactly whose side they would take and it wasn't ours. We didn't try to con them because we couldn't. They knew we were kids and what we'd try to get away with.

It's different now. Some parents are their kid's friends. "My son or daughter doesn't lie." Give me a break. "Don't discipline *my* child—you'll hurt the child's feelings." Discipline is something that must be forced on a child because if they never learn it from the outside they will never develop it from the inside. You're getting too deep, Jeri.

"What?" I said. "Do you want another beer?" "Oh yeah, one and done." "Yeah, I heard that before. You're not from around here are you?" "No, just passing through." "I thought so. You don't talk like you're from around here. Where are you headed?" "I'm on my way to York, PA. I used to have friends in this area but I guess they moved out." "That'll be seventy-five cents." "Oh yeah, sorry." Funny, I didn't notice the price of the first one. Seventy-five cent drafts! That's a far cry from the last time I had a beer here. Quarter drafts then. Oh well, I'll finish this one and leave. Don't feel much like talking or drinking.

Man, I wish I could go back in time, back to the time when I didn't have to make decisions. The hardest things I had to do were shovel the sidewalk, cut hedges and grass, fill the coal bin and take out ashes. That was hard enough. I'd be out in the backyard fooling around. I'd see Pop's truck coming down the alley, the front wheels barely on the ground, the bed of the truck heaping full of coal. I knew what was coming next. "Well, Guy, we got a load of coal to unload," which translated from Pop language to son language, meant, "You better get a move on, son, you can get it done before dark." I have very powerful shoulders that were developed because of these little chores, like shoveling coal into buckets that held thirty-five pounds apiece. Picking them up, one in each hand, required me to shrug my shoulders to get them off the ground. I carried them through the yard, down the back cellar stairs to the coal bin. The coal had bits and pieces of slate and debris in it, so it had to be strained.

Our dog, Inky, a little black cocker spaniel, was afraid to go outside the house. Inky had a rather unpleasant incident with a cat when she was a puppy. She started chasing a cat, the cat got irritated, turned and scratched her nose with its claws. Inky decided the house was safe; outside was dangerous. Inky used the coal bin to do her business.

Shoveling and straining coal was a daily chore for me. We had a stoker with a coal hopper. This hopper had to be filled every night. There was a grate on top of the hopper. I'd take a bucket of coal, dump it on the grate and strain it, removing nails, pieces of wood, slate and dog shit. I guess you could call it a shitty job.

If you burn coal, there are always ashes. That was another chore, carrying out the ashes. We had four metal tubs, each shaped to fit under the firepit of the stoker. Every night I came out of the cellar with coal dust all over me. It's a wonder I never developed miner's asthma. Some nights the black coal dust was offset by the fine white powdery ash, creating a kind of salt and pepper effect. The ashes were picked up once a week by the town truck.

The ashes had many uses. Some people used them in their gardens to grow tomatoes. I'd dump them in the holes in the alley along the house. We spread them on the street in winter to prevent slipping. It was hard to get stuck in the snow; too many coal fires, too much coal ash. It made a great skid retardant. Kids used ashes to sharpen the runners of their sleds. The ashes blended with the white of the snow; the coal dust did not.

As a kid, I thought snow naturally turned black after a few days. It was that same coal dust that robbed so many miners of their breaths and eventually their lives. Miner's asthma, black lung disease, ciliosis, whatever it was called, it was a killer. I can remember miners whose hands were engrained with fine black powder. When I was a kid, I'd sit on the front porch with Mr. White, our next-door neighbor. He'd tell me stories about working as a shaker boy when he was only nine years old. His days as a miner were cut short by miner's asthma. He couldn't sleep lying down. His lungs would fill with fluid. He slept sitting at a table with his head on the table as though it were a pillow. Coal: the provider, the destroyer.

Coal provided food, clothing, shelter and a little spending money. Coal took health, limbs and lives. I remember Jim McAndrews' uncle, a twenty-five-year-old man with young children, being carried out of the mines, his life crushed out of him in a cave-in. Pop used to tell me stories of miners who were trapped for days on end in those tunnels which were barely high enough to stand in. After they ran out of water and food, they would urinate on the bark of the shoring and eat the bark to stay alive. He told me about working with a guy one day when a slab of rock fell on the guy's gloved hand. After a few minutes he turned to my dad and said, "Doc, my hand feels sweaty and weak." He took the glove off his injured hand; his ring and middle fingers remained in the glove, pinched off cleanly by the rock. What I had to do as a child paled in comparison to what men like my father and Mr. White faced growing up.

⌛

I'd better move; these two beers are starting to get to me. I should have eaten something before I left York. "You sure you don't want another beer, buddy?" "No thanks, I'd best be off." "Okay, pal, stop again if you're in the area." "I'll do that." Damn, I hate coming out into bright light. I can't stop sneezing. Well Jeri, here you stand in the middle of Main Street blinded by the light and sneezing like someone with hay fever during harvest time. I've got to blow my nose. Hey Jeri, here's an idea. Why don't you use your arm like you did when you were a kid? Yeah, God's earliest handkerchief. No one is around so just blow out your nose. I can hear the kids I teach. "Oh, gross." Ah, the mundane things of life. Learning by life's experiences.

I was on my way home one night from Lenny Leed's after finishing a frosted mug of root beer. The evening was mild for January. I passed Clioris Bar, which was next to where Bart Barry used to live before his house was torn down. The hedges in front of what once was a house remained intact. As I passed the hedges, I noticed what I thought was an icicle hanging from the hedges. Without thinking about the lack of icicles anywhere else, I grabbed the frozen stick of ice, only it wasn't ice. God, did I get sick. It took me a long time before I could pass that hedge without gagging. Geez, Jeri, why the pleasant thoughts?

Main Street. Good old Main Street. Think I'll walk "uptown," to see what if anything has changed.

Blackthorne and Main, Fallon's Store no longer there, Hoolahan's house, across from Fallon's, is still there. Across the street on the other two corners are the American Legion and Clem's Bar. As a kid, I saw the inside of only a few bars, and those only at Halloween. We'd hit the bars, do our song and dance, get some money from the men at the bar and leave. I remember Clem's. It was an old-fashioned bar with sawdust on the floor. A lot of old miners used to patronize it. Many miners chewed tobacco since it was too dangerous to smoke in the mines. After working up a good chew between sips of beer, they'd spit the juice on the floor. The sawdust absorbed it, which made cleaning the floor easier.

Standing on the corner, looking up Blackthorne Street toward the McDowells' house way up at the top, I can still see traces of a path. We used that path to walk to the dam. The dam, or New Rail Dam as it was called, was a great place to swim, at least we thought so. I imagine today it would be considered too dirty and unclean to swim in, but to us it was a swimmer's paradise.

We were like little nomad kids. We learned the route from our elders, or in our case, older brothers, sisters and neighbors. Like Pied Pipers, they led us out of town through the forest and up to the dam. Through repetition, the route became part of our common store of knowledge. Every trip was an adventure. Word would pass from neighborhood to neighborhood. "We're going to the dam. Ya wanna come?"

Sometimes as many as twelve or more of us would make our way out of Pleasant Dale up to the woods through the tunnel under the highway known as the Pleasant Dale

Bypass and past the Rizzi. The Rizzi was a pond. We never knew how it got its name, but we were warned by brothers and sisters, "Never, ever swim in the Riz." It contained snakes, frogs and the dreaded sinkholes. These sinkholes were known to drag unsuspecting people to their deaths. So fearsome was the legend of the sinkholes and the stories of unknown kids who perished there that none of us ever tempted fate. We gave the Riz a wide berth. Occasionally, as we got older, we would take our BB guns and shoot at the tadpoles, but we never swam there. Once past the Riz, we hiked through woods until we reached the perimeter of the Scranton-Wilkes Barre Airport.

If we sneaked under the fence and crossed the airport runways it cut at least a half hour off the hiking time, but crossing the airport was both illegal and dangerous. Of course, we were forbidden to cross the airport. When older brothers and sisters were stuck with the task of taking us swimming with them, they avoided the airport. When they were not burdened with us they threw caution to the wind and crossed the forbidden runways. Like all fences, the fences that surrounded the airport presented few real obstacles to determined kids in search of adventure. Crossing the airport became a rite of passage. Advice from those who successfully made this crossing was heeded carefully. After all, they'd been there. "Remember run across the runways, keep low and always look for the red devil." When spotted by the red devil, throw caution to the wind, run like hell to the nearest fence and duck safely into the woods. Few kids were ever caught. After all, a frightened kid is a fast kid. One bright warm July day, the call went out: Let's go to the dam.

The plan set in motion a long series of "Mrs. Grady, can Joe go swim with us?" "Did your mother say it was okay?" "Yes, Mrs. Grady." That exchange was followed by a quick trip to my house. "Mrs. Docerty, can Jeri go swimming with us?" "Did your mother say you could go?" "Yes, Mrs. Docerty." And so it went, house after house, permission after permission until there was me, Sean, Joe, Jim, Spike, most of the Breslin brothers and Tom McDowell, whose house we would have to pass on the way to the dam. One day Bobby O'Rourke joined us. Bobby lived across town from us so he very seldom played with us. Bobby was the smartest kid in our class, Tom McDowell the second smartest. Bobby was at Tom's house that day, so he joined our expedition. This was to be a very eventful day, a day none of us would ever forget, for it was on that day we took our first shortcut across the airport. We all agreed it was worth the chance. After all, we might add as much as an hour to our swimming time, a half hour off the trip up and if all went well we'd cut another half hour off on our way back.

We set off in high spirits; our steps were quick and light. We were young, full of life and more importantly, we had a goal. Most of us were excited, not just because we were going swimming, but also because we decided finally to cross the airport. For us that was another step toward whatever we figured maturity to be at the age of ten. That stirred us, that's what had our juices flowing, our hearts pounding and our feet carrying us along at a much faster pace than normal. We were about to cross more than the airport runways. We were about to become experienced. Now most of us agreed that this would be our course. One of our members was hesitant. Bobby O'Rourke brought up some good points, logical reasons why our actions would be sheer folly. First, we'd get caught. Secondly, it really is dangerous. Third, it's not that much shorter. We could walk faster and make up the half hour. Fourth, he was scared. Fifth, we'd get caught. We listened. After all, Bobby was the smartest kid we knew, aside from Tom McDowell. Then, we politely told Bobby he was full of shit and if he didn't want to come with us he could go home and swim in his bathtub. Reluctantly and under pressure, he agreed.

Thinking back on the episode, I realize Bobby was right, but still full of shit. The trip seemed to fly by. We passed now familiar places without much notice. Then, looming in front of us was the embankment. It marked the edge of the airport. There atop that hill was the fence, the first obstacle in our path. We ran, crouched, to the top, then spread right and left looking for a place to crawl under the fence. We were like commandos on a secret mission. Kids are like rats; they can crawl through spaces that are much smaller than the girth of their bodies. It didn't take long before Tucker Breslin found a spot and was on the other side. "Over here," he whispered. Except for Bobby, quickly we followed. Once more, in a desperate voice, Bobby pleaded his case. Too late. In our minds we were faster than the wind, more cunning than a fox, we were invincible. One quality we weren't gifted with was intelligence. Okay, Bobby had it, but Bobby didn't count. Tom McDowell had it, but Tom was with us. We were able to help Bobby under the fence.

We made the first runway quickly. We sprinted across. Geez, this is a piece of cake. Our pace slowed. We were getting cocky. What red devil? By the time we reached the second runway, we were no longer bunched up. Bravado had taken over. We were taking our good old time. Someone, I can't remember who, mentioned seeing a yellow pickup truck heading toward us. "Hey," Spike said, "it's not red; why worry?" We didn't. We were crossing the second runway on an angle towards the fence nearest the woods. We'd be able to pick up the trail to the dam somewhere around there. There was a gully between us and the fence; I remember that clearly. Right about then someone yelled, "Jesus, that pickup is coming at us fast."

It was on us before we knew it. I still can't figure out how it got to us as quickly as it did. Two men got out of the truck running and waving pistols in the air. "Holy shit," someone yelled. We were off like frightened gazelles. The men were like lions that spotted the slowest and the most confused of us and that was Bobby. His worst nightmare came true. These guys were never going to catch us. They were too fat, too slow, too winded. Then, just as we reached the gully, we heard two loud pops, like firecrackers but louder. Someone yelled, "Oh Christ, they're shooting at us." That's all we needed to hear; we kicked in the afterburners, cleared the ditch, made the fence and were on the other side in a time that would have made any Olympic sprinting coach sit up and take notice.

All but one made it. Bobby had stopped. It was as though he couldn't believe it, like a frightened rabbit. We yelled encouragement but it was too late. The ditch was his downfall. He gave up. One of the men grabbed him. The other approached the fence. "Come on out or we'll shoot your buddy." Man, we were scared. The other man yelled, "You've got two minutes." Bobby was white as a ghost. We huddled. The conversation went back and forth, "Leave him; let's get out of here." "No, you can't do that; they'll shoot him." "Come on let's get out of here." The discussion might just as well not have happened. We knew we couldn't just leave him there. What if it were one of us? Someone brought up a good point. "Bobby always helps us with our homework." That did it, we came out. God, were we in trouble.

I know now that those men weren't using real bullets, probably blanks they used to frighten birds away from the airport. We didn't know that then. Besides none of us wanted Bobby's death on our conscience. That would have been a major mortal sin. So we came out of hiding, crawled back under the fence and went to face the music.

They loaded us into the back of the pickup truck, a yellow not a red pickup truck, and drove us back to a building. There they asked us our names and where we lived. Then they locked us in a room. We were too scared to talk, or cry, or for that matter anything else. What was going through our minds was too horrible to even talk about. A judge, then reform school or St. Michael's School for wayward boys. That was the worst-case scenario. The best we could hope for was, "Wait till your father gets home." That's what really scared the hell out of us.

After what seemed like a year, the door finally opened. The heavier of the two men from the truck came in, and with him was George Michaels. George Michaels was the chief of police from Pleasant Dale. Oh Lord, our silent prayers to St. Jude, the patron saint of lost causes, had fallen on deaf ears. We're headed up the river for sure, either Kris Lynn or St. Michael's, both reform schools. We were numb, dumbfounded, we couldn't speak.

Chief George was truly a man to be reckoned with. He was tough, a former professional boxer and coal miner. The chief was big and burly, and it was a well-known fact that he took crap from no one. "Get moving boys." I don't know about anybody else, but my legs were shaking. I could hardly stand, let alone walk. He herded us out to the police car. There he piled most of us into the backseat and crammed the rest into the front next to him. I was lucky. I was jammed into the back. The drive into town was much too quick. The chief drove into the alley in back of the police station, got us out of the car then marched us through the back door of the station. The only thing he said in a very stern, cold voice was, "Into that first cell, boys." We were like little, wet, scared puppy dogs, heads down, eyes on the floor; we started to develop a prison shuffle. Once we were in the cell, the chief shut the door. I could picture myself, day after day going through the same routine. Life. Life for crossing the airport.

To say we were disheartened would be an understatement. We just shifted around the cell nervously, not daring to talk. The chief was probably calling our mothers right now. My mom would kill me, but Pop, geez. I shuttered just thinking about it. I was not alone; we probably all felt the same. Time dragged on, it seemed like an eternity, then the door from the chief's office opened and he came out. He did not look happy. A silent "Jesus, Mary and Joseph," passed quickly through my mind. He stopped in front of the cell, looked us over, then in a deep and serious voice the chief said, "Boys, if I ever hear that you go anywhere near that airport ever again, I'll tan your hides. Then I'll make sure your dads tan your hides. Then, I'll ship you out to St. Mike's till you're too old to remember what you did. Do you understand me? Well, do you?" We spoke as one, "Yes, Chief." "Okay boys, get out of here." The chief just opened the door to the cell, which had never been locked and told us to go out the back door and go home.

Not one of us had the courage to ask the chief if he had called our moms. As it turned out, he hadn't. He had given us a huge break. Of course, we didn't know it at the time, so we were sweating bullets when we finally got home. Mom asked me if I had a good time. Oh, oh, she's setting me up. I said "Yeah," which was really a long conversation for me. Then I expected her to launch into a tirade about being the death of her, Pop getting home from work, the nuns being scandalized, Father Nilus, and the whole town knowing of her convict son, but all she said was, "Good." I still wasn't absolutely sure the chief wouldn't tell our pops. Pop got home that night, lay down for a while, ate supper and then went uptown to Lenny Leed's to shoot the breeze with his buddies. This was a critical time because Chief Michaels usually stopped in at Lenny's at night. I'm sure St. Jude, the Virgin Mary and all the saints were sick of me praying to them. Pop finally got home. He sat down for a while, didn't say anything. Then, he knelt down and said his prayers before going to bed. I joined him. He, of course, was saying the time honored, "Now I lay me down to sleep." I, however, was promising the world, my soul and all my offspring to St. Jude, the Virgin Mary and all the saints. "Thanks, thanks and thanks again." My resolve to lead an exemplary life lasted about a week. In that time period I lit numerous candles to all who answered my prayers and I lit a special one for Chief Michaels. He scared the living hell out of us but he let it go at that and all of us were forever in his debt.

It didn't keep us from crossing the airport again. The following summer we were older, "experienced," and time, the great healer, also dulls memories of the past. Besides we knew we'd never get caught again.

⧗

Those trips to the dam, the free orchard above the dam and all other adventures we pursued on foot or bike seem like figments of my imagination but they were real.

Looking back down to Main Street toward the town hall, the scene of our incarceration so many years ago, down towards Murphy's Store, a little place that sold comics, magazines, sodas and steamed hot dogs. The old Palace Theater that became a dress factory. Across the street from the old theater is the hosey.

The hosey, or the volunteer fire department, is one of the mainstays of any small town and not just in the coal regions. It was a social gathering place for the men and women who served their community. In summer, spring and early fall, the huge garage doors were always open. As you passed, you'd see the men sitting in chairs facing Main Street. Sometimes talking, sometimes playing cards, other times just sitting and looking. Most always they waved at us as we passed. Across from the hosey was Lenny's, a pool hall. Lenny Leed was a well-known pool player and often would have a nationally known pool player put on shooting demonstrations. We'd play pool, straight, eight ball or pill bottle. In pill pool, there were pills with numbers on them, everyone got a number and whoever was able to sink their ball first would win the money in the pot.

Lenny sold everything. Ice cream by the scoop, popsicles, Dixie cups, fudgesicles and ice cream sandwiches. He had every conceivable kind of soft drink: Coke, Pepsi, Neehi grape and orange, root beer, clear and regular birch beer. Lenny also sold frosted mugs of draft root beer and buttermilk, plus various local bottled beverages. He had racks of new comics and piles of used ones, baseball cards, football cards and playing cards. Lenny sold candy: Mary Janes, Baby Ruths, 5th Avenues, Three Musketeers, Mars bars, Hershey bars and so many more that I can't remember. Then, there were the long strips of red and black licorice, long pieces of waxed paper with little color sugar buttons on them, jellybeans by the bag, Sen-Sens by the handful, Life Savers and multi-colored gumdrops with sugar crystals on them. He had every kind of chewing gum: Beechnut, Juicy Fruit, cinnamon, spearmint, gum that burned you when you chewed it, sweet gum, sour gum. Jawbreakers. With all-day suckers, you really got your money's worth. No wonder we had so much energy. Lenny also sold cigarettes, cigars and chewing tobacco. He sold loose cigarettes, three for a nickel. We'd sit around on rainy days, drink soda and watch the men play pool. Around the Fourth of July, Lenny sold fireworks, anything from sparklers and black snakes to firecrackers, cherry bombs and M-80s. As kids, we saved our money to buy firecrackers. In order to finance our purchases at Lenny's, we scoured the town for returnable soda bottles: two cents for small bottles, five cents for quart bottles. We knew how to get the most for our money: penny candy, used comic books and baseball cards, which also supplied us with bubble gum. We'd split sodas or buy packs of Kool-Aid, or little wax bottles filled with some kind of orange syrup that was pure sugar. As for fireworks, packs of firecrackers broken apart and used individually provided us with hours of dangerous fun. We bought stick matches by the box, the kind of matches you could light on any kind of surface. Those matches were a lot of fun. You could drop them down the barrel of a BB gun and shoot. If the match hit something hard it would light on fire. We'd also tie matches to the front of our homemade arrows and shoot them. God, we were destructive.

One summer afternoon, around the Fourth of July, we were just fooling around, bored, clever or whatever. We decided to liven up Lenny's. Joe, Jim and I had gotten some firecrackers earlier in the week. I don't know how we learned to do this trick, but it worked really well. We decided to put a firecracker bomb under one of the chairs in Lenny's. I don't know why, it just seemed like a good idea at the time. All we needed was a pack of matches, a lit cigarette and a firecracker. You placed the fuse of the firecracker next to the head of the matches, and then the lit cigarette about an inch from the match heads. Close the matchbook cover and leave. It was the perfect time bomb.

We were hanging around the front of the store. Joe went into the bathroom, which was about halfway down the length of the pool hall. There he prepared the miniature bomb. When he walked back towards the front, he nonchalantly dropped it behind a vacant chair. As soon as he got to the front, we bid Lenny farewell and casually walked out.

Lenny's was a long narrow building. It had no side windows, just a front door and two outside large glass windows that displayed whatever Lenny wanted to get rid of and a small back door. Perfect! We figured it would just be a loud pop.

Once outside, we headed for the alley that ran the length of the building, there to wait for what we expected to be a little noise. We got to the back quickly but without drawing any undue attention to ourselves. We sat by the wall in back of Lenny's for about five minutes. "It must be a dud," Joe said. We agreed. Our prank didn't work. Oh well, there'd be other chances before we ran out of firecrackers.

We got up and headed down to the Breslins' house to see if any of the brothers were around. We had gone about ten steps or so when all of a sudden this god-awful bang sounded. "Holy shit!" Jim yelled. "Oh, oh. We've done it now, we've blown up Lenny's." We found out later that there was no damage; it just scared the hell out of some of the old guys sitting there. That little firecracker echoed through that narrow place like it was a stick of dynamite. We took off as if we'd just seen a ghost. We arrived at the Breslins' backyard out of breath, scared but elated at the same time. It took a while to catch our breath. We were all trying to talk at once. "Wait till you hear what we did." Tucker, Chuckie and Joe Breslin were truly impressed by our daring deed, but Tucker brought up something that we hadn't thought of yet. "What if Lenny knew it was you?"

I seriously don't think any of us ever thought that we'd be suspected. After all, we weren't even there when the firecracker went off. Like the proverbial light bulb that appears over your head, we lit up the yard in broad daylight. Now, why didn't we think of that? Lenny Leed after all was no dummy. Like so many pranks we pulled as kids, this one was spontaneous. Very little consideration was given to consequences, but if Lenny found us out there would be consequences. Being barred from Lenny's was like separating us from all of life's serious pleasures like candy, soda, bubble gum cards, comics, fireworks, not to mention seeing some really good pool games. Lenny also had pinball machines. We were too young to play them, since the machines paid off cash prizes, but they were in our future and thus of major interest to us.

Geez, why was life always so complicated? After all, it was only a firecracker. We didn't know it would be so loud. Well, too late now. We'd just have to wait and see what happened. Lenny was not the kind of guy who would tell our fathers outright. What he would do would be just tell us straight out not to come into his store and that would be it.

We went back the next day, not all of us just, Jim, Tucker and myself. Tucker had not been with us the day before. We just used him for diversion. We each brought a double orange popsicle, the kind you could break in half, and we were standing around the pinball machine watching one of the older guys play. He had racked up over a hundred games and was playing off the excess games to cash in at a hundred. Lenny paid a nickel a point, so the guy did all right. As we walked back over to the counter, Lenny asked Jim and I if we'd seen a couple of guys from West Pleasant Dale in the pool hall the day before. We had, in fact. One was related to Jim. "Yeah," Jim said. "I thought so," Lenny said. "Those little SOBs set off a cherry bomb in here yesterday. Christ, old Jim Duffy almost had a heart attack. Wait till I see those little, little—Never mind. Thanks boys. Here, grab a handful of gumdrops for yourselves." "Gee, thanks, Lenny."

Not only didn't we get caught, but we were rewarded for fingering the wrong kids. Both Jim and I knew his cousin could care less about coming into Lenny's, since most of the kids from West Pleasant Dale didn't hang out there anyway. In fact, Jim's cousin would love the publicity. He and his brothers were rough kids. Besides, raising hell was something the kids from that side of town did quite regularly.

As I stroll down Main Street, I realize how long ago it's been since I walked down this street. It's changed. My memories of it are now tempered by numerous small towns I've traveled through in the years since I last took this walk. One thing that strikes me as different is the lack of kids or for that matter even of adults on the street.

The house that was put up where the Barrys used to live and the town hall across the street look much the same. Clioris Bar is no more. The store next to it is also out of business. Too much competition to keep mom and pop stores going, I guess.

"Afternoon." Geez, that startled me. "Oh, hi there." I forgot that people actually say hello to strangers around here. I didn't even see her coming. Too much time looking down at the sidewalk. Get your head up, Jeri. You're liable to walk into something. Just thinking about walking into something strikes me as funny.

I can see the old Palace Theater up the street. I ran into it once. One of the reasons I used to rationalize why I never studied in high school. First semester, freshman year, Billy Moran came down to my house to help me study algebra. I should have known better. Anyway, Billy and I were studying up a storm when the question came up of whether the dog had been fed or not. Now, I gave it table scraps but it seems that was not enough. From my point of view, the dog could have gone at least a month without eating and still had a lot of body fat to live on. The command came down, "Go get the poor dog some dog food." The dog was always my dog when it came to feeding it and picking dog crap out

of the coal. "I'm studying. Billy came down to help me."
"Billy will wait, won't you Billy?" Billy had no option.
"Yeah, I'll wait." "But I gave him the scraps from supper."
"Go get *your* dog some food." Ah, shit, lost again.

Now I really did want to pass that algebra test, so despite the fact that it was snowing, and the sidewalks were slick, I hopped on my bike and headed to the A & P to get the poor dog a bone, so to speak. As I flew up Blackthorne Street and made the right on Main, my back wheel slipped. I recovered quickly. Nothing like young reflexes. I now had a straight run to the A & P. Lenny's was about the halfway point, and I was coming on Lenny's quickly. I reached Squire Muldon's house just as his wife opened their car door in front of me. Mr. Muldon got his name, "Squire," because of his position as justice of the peace. I saw the door open. Their little poodle jumped out. Now, if it hadn't been for that poodle I would have made it. But, the door, coupled with the poodle, caused me to overcompensate. I couldn't keep the bike up. I went into a slide and that's all I remember.

As I came to, I looked up. There was a crowd of people around me but the only one I recognized was Skunk Burlock. Upon seeing Skunk, I passed out again. The next time I woke up, I was on the couch at home. The Lone Ranger and his faithful Indian companion, Tonto, were on TV. I vaguely remember a "Kemosabi" and a hearty "Hi-ho, Silver." Then darkness. I woke up in Mercy Hospital in Scranton. My head hurt so bad I saw stars. I spent the next five days in the hospital, sunglasses on, head throbbing, and driving my mom nuts. My buddy, Jim, had a request played over the radio for me. I really appreciated that, but the rest of the time was spent in misery. I made a vow never to study again. See what studying did to me! It just hurt too much to study. I was pretty religious about that vow most of my high school years.

Looking at the building that had been the theater brings back memories of those Saturday afternoons spent watching Roy Rogers and the many heroes that played out those moral lessons of good triumphing over evil. In those movies the good guy always wins in the end. Dead shots, they were able to disarm villains by not only outdrawing them, but by shooting the guns out of their hands, they dashed all their hopes of attaining ill-gotten loot without the proper struggle for it. They reinforced our beliefs in right and wrong, good and evil, and what goes around comes around. These struggles, however, were not easy. Just the opposite. They were filled with about an hour and fifteen minutes of good being caught on the ropes and pummeled by evil until it was almost impossible for the heroes or heroines to survive. Then, when all appeared lost, when no possible chance of victory appeared likely, the hero reached down into his goodness and got his moral second wind and thus allowed evil to be thwarted once again. These values were taught to us at home, at school and at church. Then, with dramatic flair, they were played out for us on the silver screen, all for the mere cost of fifteen cents.

Thinking on those dramas and the serials that stretched on chapter after chapter, week after week, makes my heart run faster. The hero was always on the edge of disaster, but he never gave up. He knew that if his heart were pure, his intentions honest and his horse tried and true he'd get, but never kiss, the girl. He'd always leave her hanging, having to settle for second best while he, mounted on his only true

110

love, his horse, rode off into the sunset with his trusted but clumsy sidekick.

Gone are those days of yesteryear with everything cut and dry, black or white, no shades of gray. Westerns were not the only bill of fare that drew us to the Palace. Any movie did, with the exception of love stories, which we wrote off as a waste of time, money and an afternoon. We'd watch knights and squires battling for castles or Robin Hood fighting tyranny. Good simple comedies were, no pun intended, always good for a laugh, but what really fired us up were war movies.

John Wayne became every boy's hero. We'd fight battle after battle in that theater. There'd be all the carnage of war without the graphics and blood of today's movies. After all, what happened on the silver screen had happened for real as fathers, uncles and cousins would attest. We had been at war and the town had its share of living, dead and wounded combat veterans. These men very seldom talked of war or for that matter went to see movies of it. We, however, viewed war as a noble undertaking and played hard at imitating what we saw.

Of course, other movies taught us other virtues. Religious movies: *Moses and the Israelites*, *The Ten Commandments*, *Ben Hur*, *The Robe* and *Barabas* taught us Bible history. *Song of Bernadette* and *Miracles at Lourdes* gave us hope. Then of course there were the horror movies. Seeing some of the movies that petrified us back then makes me laugh today. Bats, wolves, ghouls and other unspeakable monsters came alive in black and white in the Palace. Hands over our eyes, fingers spread so as not to miss the goriest part, we'd sit on the edges of our seats. If we went to see these movies at night, we'd always run home not daring to look right or left and always feeling that the evil we witnessed on the screen was right in back of us.

On summer nights, fires burning, potatoes placed in a circle around the fire, hot dogs on sticks roasting, the stories of werewolves, aliens and the one armed hook-handed men who terrorized couples parked on lonely roads would make firelight cast eerie shadows across our faces as one by one we tried to scare each other to death. It was always, "Yeah, but my Uncle Tony told me about the girl on the Suscon Road, the one that got killed on the way to her prom." There were stories of hooks on car doors, girls in tattered prom dresses, the hulking hairy giant who was reported to hang out at the cemetery on nights of the full moon. Told and retold but never exactly the same. Stories that gained in stature as they became gorier were fed by grade B horror movies we'd seen at the Palace, Saturday and Sunday matinees.

Sunday's in Lent the moms in the area would make the exception to stringent Lenten rules and allow us to sneak up to the movie, out of sight of the nuns, of course. All movies were first screened through the Legion of Decency to make sure they were not either on the "objectionable in part" or "totally banned for all Catholics" list. Then there was the Thursday evening specials, where for a mere thirteen cents you could go to the 7:00 movie, provided your homework was done, and be home at 8:30. All patrons, particularly the young ones, came under the watchful eye of the movie manager, Mrs. O'Reiley. Mrs. O'Reiley, like John Wayne, gave evildoers only one last chance to straighten up and fly right. She was known to escort young ruffians out of the theater by the ears, one in each hand. The first "That will be enough of that, boys" was followed by "If I have to come down here one more time, I'll tan your hide and throw you out. Understand?" That second warning was usually enough. Mrs. O'Reiley had a memory like an elephant and once she threw you out it took a lot of groveling to work your way back into her good graces.

Eventually the Palace, like so many other small town theaters, succumbed to competition from television. Movies were still featured but now to see them you had to venture to Scranton or Pittston, which required bus fare, plus movie admission, which was a bit too costly for us. The Palace was sorely missed.

⧗

Lenny's is no longer what I remember it to be, so glancing in the once well-stocked window I pass it by. I don't feel like going inside. Age has diminished my desire for orangesicles and white birch beer. I am, however, tempted to see if they still serve buttermilk in frosted mugs. Now, Jeri, buttermilk and beer are not an ideal mix on a warm June afternoon. I need a sandwich and a cup of coffee. Those two beers have made me sluggish.

I think I remember Mary Kay telling me that the small lunch counter operated by the Breslins is still open. I think she said it was called Pleasant Dale Restaurant. Mary Kay, my sister, keeps me informed about Pleasant Dale. She still maintains close ties in town. Whatever the place is called now, that restaurant provided me with my first job.

I can't remember how old I was but I washed dishes there. Tucker Breslin and I worked a few days a week during one summer vacation. Our hours were from 11:30

to 1:00. I wasn't paid much, but I think I would have worked for nothing. The idea of having a job made me feel big and old. Tucker and I were good workers. We'd work our way through pots and pans, stacks of dishes, cups, saucers, water glasses, silverware, you name it. No job was too big or too small. The hours were right, working conditions pleasant although hot and we got a free meal at the end of our shift. Tucker's mom and pop owned the place so they were very generous with their portions of food for two loyal employees. We could have had anything on the menu, but we usually got one of two basics: hamburger with lettuce and tomato and onion or two chilidogs, each with French fries.

My experience with French fries was limited to Mom's oven baked fries or those greasy, salt-ladened fries we'd get at Rocky Glen Park. There never was a serious choice as to whose were best. Rocky Glen French fries were absolutely the best French fries. I think their secret was never to change the grease because as summer got close to ending, the fries got better and better. Most of us kids were traditionalists, that is, we liked salty French fries dipped in catsup. Sometimes we'd put a few dashes of vinegar on the fries for variety. That was my experience with fries before I worked at the Breslins'.

It was while working for the Breslins that summer that I was introduced to French fries smothered in gravy with just a dash or two of catsup for added flavor. God, they were good. I can remember scarfing down a whole plate of fries, and then dipping my hamburger into the leftover gravy. My mouth waters just thinking of it. Today's nutrition standards concerning what's good and bad for the human body tell me that whatever I like is either fattening, illegal, or immoral. Those post-work meals were all of those. Loaded with fatty grease, they were so good they had to be illegal and there was so much food that I had to be committing the sin of gluttony just eating all of it. We were absolved, however, by Tucker's grandmother, who encouraged us to eat everything on our plates. "After all, you are growing boys, and remember there are people starving in China." Of course, most grandmothers advised us to eat, but that "there are people starving in China" was usually reserved for beets, broccoli or some other equally colorful but tasteless pile of food that tasted as bad as it was good for you.

⧗

Even though my sister, Mary Kay, keeps in touch with people from town, so far I don't think I've recognized anybody. I've only seen a few people and none of their faces rings a bell. Main Street USA. Walking, looking and thinking. If I were walking in downtown York, I'd be alert and aware. Here I feel comfortable, relaxed and at ease. What was so much a part of me at one time just seems to slip back into me like the warm feeling you get when someone you like but haven't seen for while suddenly pops up from out of nowhere. I feel like that little redheaded kid on an errand for my mom. The only difference, aside from age and size, is the fact I'm not in any real hurry. I no longer clutch notes reminding me of what Mom wanted. I can forget all by myself and I usually do. Even today I'll walk into a store specifically to buy one item. I'll leave with five, none of which is the item I went into the store for. I get as mad at myself as my mom used to get at me. I guess that old saying is true, "The more things change the more they remain the same."

The Main and Grove Street intersection is just up the street. That's where the restaurant should be. I really haven't paid much attention to anything since Lenny's. Goosey Haddon's, Martha's, and a few bars just kind of passed by. Martha's was a place we used to hang out when we were in high school. Goosey's was another teen hangout, but Goosey's attracted kids from out of town. It was a place where fights often broke out. Most kids I hung out with stayed around Martha's avoiding a whole lot of unnecessary problems.

The restaurant still has the lunch counter, booths on the side and tables in the back. Not too many people here, but at 3:30 in the afternoon it's an off time. I left the cemetery around 9:30, I think. Probably should get the motel room for another night. Maybe go barhopping tonight. I really just intended to visit the graves and then head back to York. Best laid plans of mice and men often do something. I guess mine have.

The menu has a little more variety to it than it had when I worked there, but my mind was made up before I even came in the door. "Hamburger with lettuce, tomato and onion, a large order of fries with gravy and a cup of coffee, please. Wait, Miss, is the coffee fresh?" "I just made it about an hour ago." "Never mind then. Give me a large Diet Coke."

The waitress seems to be about eighteen. Christ, she probably is the daughter of someone I know. She's a nice looking kid. I really loved the look she gave me when I ordered Diet Coke. She had that same expression I get when I watch someone in a supermarket put a gallon of ice cream, a large cake and a box of chocolate chip cookies on the conveyor belt, followed by two quarts of Diet Pepsi and a pack of sugarless gum. Why bother? Why not get regular Pepsi and some real gum. Go for the gusto.

There's not much on the old jukebox. Some country western, a little heavy metal. Must be for the young crowd. Some pop music for the more sedate, but nothing that appeals to me. I hate waiting for food. I feel like eating and moving. Better sit back down, Jeri. I feel self-conscious, maybe because I'm dressed in shorts, an old "I hiked the Canyon" T-shirt and a pair of racked out Nikes. I'm probably a little dirty from hiking around the coal piles and the tracks. I have the counter all to myself. There's a guy reading the paper at the back table and a young couple sitting in the booth to the back and right of me. I shouldn't feel self-conscious. Aside from the waitress nobody even bothered to glance at me. So much for making an impression, huh, Jeri?

Finally, here she comes with my grub. Hamburger looks decent enough, fries smothered in gravy. The glass of Coke could be larger. "Can I get you anything else, sir?" "Yes, can I have some catsup?" "It's right in front of you, sir." "Oh." Shit, I hate being an idiot. I know why I didn't see it. It was hiding in the red Heinz fifty-seven variety bottle. Anyone could miss that, right Hawkeye? I hate catsup bottles. Shake and shake and it all comes out in a big blob.

I can't finish all this food. What's the matter, Jeri, eyes bigger than your stomach? Too warm, too humid to enjoy this heavy a meal. I probably could have gotten by on a Coke and a tuna or chicken sandwich. "Is the food okay, sir?" "Oh it's great, I'm just not as hungry as I thought." "Do you want anything else?" "No, just the check. I have to get going." It's a good thing I stopped at the MAC machine before I went to the cemetery this morning. I'd better get moving; the food is making me sleepy. If I had the van with me, I'd probably head back to the motel for a nap.

⧗

Back to the sunlight. No sneezes this time. The restaurant was not as dark inside as the bar. Where to go next? I could walk the length of Main Street to the road that leads into the spot where O'Brian's Bowling Alley used to be and then walk the alley back along the tracks. That would take me back to the fields we used to play in as a kid. Back to Winter Street, back past Jim's, Tucker's, Sean's old houses. Back past St. Marie's. Either way I'll walk down at least as far as O'Brian's then make up my mind.

Feels good to be walking again. The Pleasant Dale Bank is still impressive as ever. Built in the style of the post office and government buildings, it's a symbol of conservation, strength, stability. A no-nonsense place to do business, it emotes trust. I put many a quarter, then a dollar a week in that bank, my Christmas club savings. Week after week my little passbook was stamped with the amount deposited. We patiently saved for that glorious day in early December when the product of our thrift was returned to us, with no interest of course, just in time to buy Christmas presents for all who were near and dear to us. We knew this to be the best method of saving for Christmas. Piggy banks were too convenient and too easy to rob. Often we'd take our own money to use ourselves or to loan to older brothers or sisters. The bank simply would not give you your money until December. They didn't allow you to dilly-dally with your deposits either. If it was a quarter a week, you deposited a quarter a week. If you missed a week you were expected to double up the following week. You complied with their rules or they wouldn't renew your Christmas club status the following year.

Petrie's Bar is next to the bank. I tended bar and did clean up work there when I was in college. Chick and Anne Petrie were pretty good to me. Good people to work for. They always had a room upstairs for me if I needed to stay over on a Friday or Saturday night.

Maybe I won't walk down to O'Brien's. I'll just go down between Petrie's and the house next door. I feel like getting off Main Street. Not much lure for me in that direction but for O'Brien's. O'Brien's was an eight lane bowling alley. Unlike bowling alleys of today, O'Brien's was small and the pins had to be set by hand. I worked at O'Brien's for about three weeks. God, what a job. My first day, they showed me the ropes and gave me one alley to run all by myself. I learned that no matter what kind of physical condition you're in, each job has its own set of unusual muscles. Hopping, bending, stretching, lifting, twice a frame for each bowler, over and over, hour after hour. It didn't faze me at the start. I was too concerned with keeping track of the games, clearing pins, sending the ball back and getting out of the way. Getting out of the way was important. I didn't need to be reminded that bowling balls were heavy; I was lifting them. Some of the bowlers could really throw that ball, while others, usually men, would use a deceptively light black ball and whip that thing down the alley. It seemed to impress their girlfriends. I'd be down in that pit clearing pins, then I'd hear a thud, followed by the distinctive noise of a bowling ball making its way down the alley.

I'd look up. "Holy shit, is this guy trying to kill me?" One or two guys used to play this game, bowling for pin boys.

The job was hard work, but it was educational. I worked with a kid who taught me how to use an ordinary drinking straw, a straight pin and some toilet paper to make my own miniature blowgun. It was probably my second day at work. I was down in the pit clearing pins when all of a sudden I felt a sting. I thought I was stung by a bee. I hopped back to the bench where I sat rubbing my butt. After about three of these little stings, it finally dawned on me that I was the butt of a joke, no pun intended. The kid showed me how he made the little blowguns. We played games of darts whenever the alleys were slow. That kid was the reason I quit setting pins. It was about 5:30 on a Sunday afternoon. He was working two alleys over from me when I heard him yell. When I looked over he was holding his mouth. Blood was seeping out from between his fingers. A wild pin caught him right smack in the mouth. It knocked two of his teeth out. That was it for me. I kind of like to smile and preferred to show teeth rather than gums when I did. I finished my games, then told the manager of my decision. He was not happy. It would leave him shorthanded, but I figured better him shorthanded than me short of teeth. Thus ended my days as a pin boy. Funny thing, the kid that got hit in the mouth was back to work a few days later. I guess he figured he had nothing more to lose. Oh-oh, did I make a little joke? You're so clever, Jeri.

I'm not walking up to O'Brien's. I really don't care if it is still open. I never really spent that much time at that end of town at least not until I got to high school. The football coach at Pleasant Dale High School lived up on the corner of Main and McAlpine Streets. I used to hang out with his daughters when I was in high school.

It was also at that intersection that a bunch of heroes from another town hopped out of a car and proceeded to beat the crap out of me. I was fifteen at the time. The football team I played on, St. Jerome's High School, won our league championship that year. I was wearing my championship jacket. I surmise those four or five brave young men took offense at me and my jacket. I remember someone from behind me yelling that I was a f——ing wise guy. I turned and was greeted by a hard right to the left eye. I hit the ground; they proceeded to do a polka on my prone body. Luckily, a woman across the street saw what was happening and threatened them with police action. After that, they hopped in their souped-up car and sped off into the sunset, as all true heroes do. That particular incident both embarrassed and humiliated me. I was a frightened little kid who made a vow that I would never be caught unprepared again. That began a lifelong interest in self-defense and the martial arts.

I'm not a violent person, but if there's one thing that gets me it's when I think of that incident. I can feel my anger well up inside me. I hate bullies, always have and I guess I always will. I guess some people enjoy the idea of beating the crap out of someone but I'm not one of them. Thinking back on it now, it probably was a valuable lesson I learned that day. It directed me towards a form of discipline that taught patience, self-control, inner peace and confidence. I learned mind over matter can serve one well. So really I should be thankful to that carload of rough riders for it was their heroics that Sunday afternoon that nudged me down another path less traveled.

⧗

Man, my mind races at times. Some days I have to think hard to remember my phone number but it seems that some things from the past just appear, and appear so vividly. That was and still is a vivid memory. The school of hard knocks, huh, Jeri?

The memory makes me turn away, back toward Grove Street. Grove Street leads back to the tracks, back to the valley, or should I say valleys: the Old Valley and the New Valley. The Old Field and the New Field. I can't really remember why anything was named as it was. Names passed from sibling to sibling, year after year, as if they were learned by osmosis. Grove Street led to the alley, which could take me home from Breslin's Diner after work, or to the back of Lenny Leed's. It led past the house where two alcoholic parents neglected their eight or nine kids. Poor kids, kids with whom I went to school.

I remember walking home through the alley one evening and seeing both of the parents passed out against a fence and one of the older girls trying to get them to wake up. Christ, I haven't thought of that since the day it happened. I felt sorry for the girl, so poorly dressed. She had eyes red from crying, her hair was unkempt, her dress ragged and dirty. I don't know how old I was at the time, but I took off running, maybe subconsciously wanting to escape the sadness. I knew she and her brothers and sisters couldn't. Maybe I just wanted to get home to my mom and pop, who might yell at me when I messed up but who fed me, clothed me, took me fishing and sat up with me when I was sick. Maybe that's why I ran. That was an awful sight.

Later the kids were taken away. The girls put in a foster home; the boys sent to St. Michael's Catholic Home for Boys. At that moment, in that alley, that evening I lit a candle in my mind for all that I had. It really wasn't all sunshine and roses in Pleasant Dale, but the good memories far outweighed the bad.

Grove Street ends straight ahead. It just disappears. The road makes a right-angled right turn. There it changes to Winter Street. At that bend on the right was, but is no more, a small machine shop. Kraft's Mill I think it was called. We'd venture there on Saturday afternoons when the mill was closed. The mill's scrap pile was at the side of the building. It was a veritable treasure trove with scrap metal objects of all kinds. The most dangerous were the curled pieces of metal, like the coiled strip from an opened can of ham. Pieces of solid metal were also found in the pile. The trick was to retrieve them without slicing our little hands into lunchmeat. The pieces of solid iron were like gold nuggets to us. They had no practical purpose. We didn't use them for anything, just hoarded them like Ali Baba's treasure. I wonder what happened to my collection. It probably went the way of my baseball cards.

Jim, Sean, Joe, Tucker, Spike and I used to pass the mill on our way to nowhere special, just to wherever. The smell of oil and machinery lingered around the place. We'd peek in the windows and see the men working at the lathes. We didn't know what they were making, but we envisioned ourselves working at those machines as fully-grown men. We felt the promise of things to come.

So many of our dreams involved the future. Going into the army, navy, marines or air force like all the other guys before us. When home on leave at Christmas, they wore their uniforms proudly. They felt proud to serve their country as their fathers and uncles had before them. We'd dream of faraway places, of adventures even beyond our wildest dreams, of armed conflict, war. We'd be heroes much like the ones we saw on the silver screen at the Palace Theater.

Then, as quickly as our visions came, they went and we were headed off again, as I am now, toward the New Valley. The New Valley is, however, no more. Landfill and houses replaced it. As I look at these houses, they seem to vanish before my eyes and in their place I see the valleys again, just as they were years ago, the same valleys we spent hours and hours playing in.

A ridge separated the New and Old Valleys, creating two almost equal depressions in the earth. Directly to the rear of the valleys was an embankment, below it a small rivulet made its way toward the sewer at the bottom of Blackthorne Street. Its waters were lifeless because of the high acidity level. Beyond the dead stream another embankment formed the railroad bed. Across the tracks were the old burnt out coal dumps. It felt strange running through the dumps, hearing the crunch of porous ashes beneath our feet. Like running on Styrofoam pellets or walking on powdered snow.

Even though these valleys were side by side, they were very different places. The New Valley was a grassy depression with trees surrounding three quarters of it. Many a knightly adventure took place there. We draped homemade bows and arrows and cardboard quivers over our shoulders. In our left hands we held shields made of wood nailed together and held fast on our arms with rope. A wood sword made from a fallen tree branch placed in our belts almost completed our array of weapons, and sometimes we'd lash pieces of cardboard to our bodies. These strips represented armor to ward off stray arrows and sword thrusts. Lances were fashioned from discarded broom handles. The would-be lances also served as fearless war horses on which we rode into battle, our mouths drooling from the clippity-clopping noises the imaginary steeds' hooves made on the ground. In this valley, fierce but harmless battles were waged. Arrows bounding off the shields and cardboard armor and loud thuds and cracks would be heard across the valley as we flayed at each other's upraised shields.

The battle plan was simple and direct. First, the attackers unleashed a volley of arrows at the defenders, who in turn lowered their shields and returned fire, volley after volley until the arrows were expended. The attackers then charged the ridge. Yells and screams, intermixed with the clippity clops and "Die Saxon pigs" or "Norman dogs." Drool and spit flew from our mouths as words, screams and clippity-clops became an unintelligible gurgling torrent of noise. Once we closed with the enemy, swords clashed. We fought shield on shield and swords on shields in a mock battle worthy of any modern day Renaissance fair.

These battles lasted as long as our energy. The battles were not without injury; accidents happen. Occasionally during a battle an honest to God scream of pain erupted as one of the combatants lost a small chunk of skin from an unprotected hand or an arrow struck an exposed part of the body. Case in point. I fired an arrow at Spike's upraised shield, the chivalrous thing to do. Spike, however, dropped his shield a little too soon causing the arrow to hit the top of the shield, where it glanced off and stuck momentarily in Spike's forehead. Never did the motherly warning, "You'll poke your eye out," ring truer than at that instance. The arrow struck about an inch above Spike's eyebrow. I heard myself gasp and then yell, "Spike, you shithead, why did you drop your shield?" Good play, Jeri, shift the blame. Spike, undaunted, simply said, "Oh yeah, well it didn't hurt none." Which in Spike's case I'm sure meant it really didn't hurt none. Spike seemed to have a real tolerance for pain.

It was no accident that we held our feudalistic battles in New Valley since Old Valley was the major source of our arrow supply. Our arrow supply grew abundantly in the Old Valley. They were made from straight, fibrous reeds that grew wild in its marshy confines. We simply pulled them out of the ground, knocked the dirt off the roots, then cut the excess off and we were in business. These arrows flew straight and sure. One arrow lasted a week or more in constant use.

Bows were no real problem to make, any relatively springy sapling or freshly cut tree branch served our purpose well. Then a penknife was used to cut away any excess twigs or small protrusions from our long bows. A small notch was cut on each end to attach a stout piece of string. The bow was complete.

We only ventured into Old Valley to restock our supplies of arrows. Old Valley was an uninviting place, a marsh-like area covered with picker bushes. It provided an excellent environment for rats, small snakes and other equally unappealing things. It had been a small dumpsite at one time. Reeds, broken bottles, and rusted cans were just part of that world. It was those god-awful picker bushes we hated. Not the kind of nettles that had two little points on them, the kind that reminded me of paramecium with horns, but the miniatures, spiked like marbles. I mean when those little suckers stuck to us, it was a real job to get them off. We felt them rasping our skin even when we were wearing heavy jeans or pants. God forbid they ever got stuck in our hair. It was next to impossible to remove them, so moms ended up cutting them out. This left us with a tell-tale bald spot, the kind kids who split their scalps or got gum stuck in their hair had. The difference was one left a scar, the other didn't. Either way the other kids constantly reminded the partly bald kid of his hair loss.

What made the trip into the Old Valley nerve-racking was the spiders and snakes. I don't know about any of the other guys but when it came to spiders and snakes, my skin crawled. Spiders weave webs, webs that are nearly invisible to the human eye. A running boy, intent on whatever he may be intent on, never really notices the web until it's wrapped securely around his face and head. Now, where there's a web, there are spiders. So the moment I felt the web wrapped around my head, my imagination kicked in. Spiders could be anywhere on or in my body, mouth, ears, nose or even in those places covered by clothes. "Oh shit, get them off, get them off." Blank stares. Docerty has finally gone over the edge. "Help me." "Help you what?" "Spiders, are there any spiders on me?" "Yeah, there's one." Whack. I left myself open. I'm fair game. Like having a birthday, guys got to hit me and hit me they did. The first couple of slaps I thought, "Thanks guys." Then the old light bulb clicked on. "Okay, okay, I think you got them." "Nah, there's another one." Whack. Me and my big mouth. I'd have sustained fewer injuries from the spiders than I would have from my friends.

The New Valley was more than a mock battlefield where young knights fought valiantly, where courageous marines stormed enemy machine gun nests or cowboys fought Indians for control of the make-believe western plains. The valley was a refuge, a place sheltered from prying eyes. Many a restful summer afternoon was spent in silence watching clouds play out young fantasies. The clouds could be horses stampeding through high fields of white grass. The clouds drifting in the heavens encouraged our active young imaginations. No one ever saw the same thing, but we all saw something. Angels with wings fluttering ever so slowly, maybe carrying some poor soul to heaven. Like dreams in the night, the clouds shifted from angels to profiles of old men or women and then became huge puffs of Indian smoke signals. Sometimes we'd drift off to sleep, sometimes not. We had learned from past meditations that what we saw was ours and ours alone. No use trying to explain where the angel, horse or the profile of Sister Bertha was located, for it existed only in the eyes of that particular daydreamer. Those afternoons were some of the most peaceful moments of our young lives. Here, we were engulfed in silence and in this silence we lived out our imaginary futures. Our lives stretched out in the naiveté of youth, all bright spots. No tears of sorrow. No failures or disappointments. Our successes, our victories flowed through our minds as wistfully as the changing clouds that created images in our imagination. God, I don't think I've felt as relaxed and in control of my life as I did then. These silent hours gave us energy, but like so many things of youth they were gone too quickly.

As peaceful as the valley was for us, it also drew the local drunks who sought the valley much for the same reasons we did. Their dreams and visions were not the same as ours. Alcoholic hazes clouded their imaginations, for their spirits were beaten down. Could this be the same path we must follow when our time comes? When they saw clouds, they were clouds. We drifted off to sleep; they passed out. The "bottle gang" we called them.

Whenever our paths crossed it usually was at the New Valley. They came into our territory and took over our land. Wars were waged for much the same reason. We resented their presence. They threw old jugs of wine and empty fifths of Four Roses whiskey everywhere. They crapped in the valley and generally stunk up the place. Their intrusions generally went unnoticed, but we always knew when they had violated the sanctity of the valley. We cleaned up after them. Amazing. We never cleaned up our rooms, desks or anything else for that matter, but we cleaned up after them. It happened one too many times. It all came to a head the day Tucker's little brother Billy fell face first into a pile of wino shit. The poor kid got sick as a dog. We consoled him, from a distance, as best we could. It seemed that the Breslin boys, or at least Billy, the younger brother, had the shittiest luck. The incident called for a council of war.

Word spread quickly. "Breslin's backyard. Now." Those of us who were in the valley at the time spread out in all directions. I sped off to Lenny Leed's. Tucker searched Winter Street. Spike headed to Grady's backyard. Forty-five minutes later approximately fifteen young warriors arrived, anxious to do battle. We were chomping at the bit. Tucker took control of the war council. After some yelling and screaming, he calmed the meeting down. We agreed. We must develop a plan. After various suggestions were proposed and rejected, Tom McDowell stood and spoke. Now Tom was the second smartest kid we knew, his intellectual ability was surpassed only by Bobby O'Rourke, who had not been seen since the airport incident.

Tom's plan was rather simple. First, we needed to scout the valley on a rotating basis. We'd all take turns. Scouts would maintain a vigil every day except Sunday. We decided to wait a week and then put our plan into action. The first scout to spot the bottle gang would sound the alarm.

Now we weren't all that dumb to go charge into a bunch of adult men. We'd stay hidden in the trees until we saw them acting stupid. In our limited experience drunkenness and stupidity went hand-in-hand, but so did meanness. Once they were drunk enough, whatever quickness and agility they had would be negated by our speed and sure-footedness.

Three weeks after the young Billy Breslin nose-dived his way to infamy, the bottle gang surfaced. Word went out rapidly. The gathering of the clan took little more than an hour. We were primed for battle but at the same time we had to maintain stealth and silence. We split into three groups, each with about five young braves intent on reenacting the "Second Battle of the Bighorn." Each group approached from a different direction. My group crossed the tracks and made our way to the burnt out coal hills west of the valley. Jim McAndrews' group came from the direction of Joe Grady's house. Before they reached the valley, they loaded up on rotten apples from Mr. Timlyn's backyard. They then slipped one by one into the Old Valley. The rotten apples were great offensive weapons. A sharpened stick was stuck into the apple, then holding the stick back by one's right hip the decaying fruit was hurled with great force. Since this was not the first time we had used rotten apples in this manner, we were fairly accurate with them.

The last group approached from Grove Street where they slipped unnoticed into the grove of trees south of the valley. Crabapple trees grew wild in this small copse. The tiny golf ball-shaped apples were capable of inflicting stinging welts when they struck unprotected skin, and believe me, we were aiming for just such areas.

My group had the neatest weapons. Our ammunition was the brainchild of Tucker Breslin. Tucker's idea was to use dog shit. Over the course of three weeks we amassed a huge pile of shit. Dog doo-doo dries hard and fast. The unappetizing mounds had reached various shades from brown to ashen gray. We used newspaper to transfer the ammo to our delivery system. Our launcher was made in the fashion of David's sling, a sling capable of slaying a giant. Surely this doo-doo delivery system was good enough to stink up a few old winos. Even though we did not think of it as poetic justice at the time, it was like an eye for an eye kind of thing. Or shit for shit. We practiced until we were good enough to hit what we aimed at.

As anxious as we were for combat, we were disciplined. Long years under Sister Bertha's tutelage taught us self-control. Our young bodies crouched. Our muscles coiled like the spring of a BB gun. We waited patiently for Tom McDowell's signal. A signal that came suddenly, as a high pitched howl, like the scream of the legendary banshee we had heard so much about, especially when our noise level reached painfully high pitches. The three-pronged attack started simultaneously. Apples, horse chestnuts and shit hit the air at the same time. The suddenness of it was truly startling. Thinking of it now makes me realize how comical it really was. We were very serious warriors avenging a wrong against us. I can close my eyes and see the absolute panic taking place in the valley at that moment.

Drunks spilled wine, brown paper bags dropped in mid-exchange. "Holy Mother of God, what the hell." "Jesus, bloody Jesus." "Holy shit." Of course, the shit was a lot less than holy. One guy got up, fell over, got up again, reached down for the wine bottle and rolled over flat on his back. Apples splatted, bouncing off bodies, dog shit hit and broke into brown and white shards of shrapnel. "Goddamn, I pissed my pants." "Get those little bastards," they screamed. One guy threw up on the somersaulted wino. We had them and we weren't letting up. The barrage intensified as our confidence level increased.

The inebriated enemy was confused, hurt and disorganized. "You little sons of bitches," one guy was yelling. All at once, as though a communal thought flashed through fifteen minds at the same time, we concentrated our fire. He never had a chance. He turned and ran as fast as his emaciated booze-soaked body could carry him. That's all we needed; they retreated in the only direction open to them, out to Winter Street. The song the "Battle of New Orleans" comes to mind: "Oh they ran through the briars and they ran through the brambles and they ran through the bushes where a rabbit couldn't go."

Victory. War whoops and cries rose from our ranks. The celebration that followed was one to be remembered. We picked up the bottles of wine and whiskey, carried them up to the railroad tracks and broke them one by one on the rails. Three half-gallons of dark red wine, one bottle of Four Roses, a pint of some white stuff that looked like water, and a quart bottle of some brownish substance, all were smashed. How many years later would it be before some of these same stout warriors would be lying about their age in pursuit of the liquid we destroyed that afternoon? The whole place stunk like Clem's Bar after a Saturday night party.

The houses, built where the valleys used to be, come back into focus. The memory of that afternoon so long ago changes as quickly as the cloud formations had when I was young. New homes block the view of that unnamed valley that angled off and then paralleled Winter Street.

⧗

Continuing up Winter Street I see a macadam alley rather than the old dirt and gravel one I remembered so well. The alley's far corner, the corner nearest the tracks, is now a backyard with a neatly kept wooden split rail fence. That yard had been home to one of the local characters of Pleasant Dale, a guy the kids knew only as old Joe Goggles.

None of the kids knew anything about old Joe. Oh, we knew he couldn't or wouldn't speak English. He was tall, but stooped over, probably from years of backbreaking labor. He was quiet and kept to himself. He lived in a crudely made shack with a corrugated tin roof. We knew he had no electricity. At night when we passed, we could see lanterns illuminating the inside of his hovel. Joe usually sat outside, except in winter. His chair was as crude as the hut he lived in. It looked more like a small wooden bench with a low railed back nailed to it.

We saw this tall, bent, gaunt-looking man struggling across the railroad tracks many times. His huge hands formed gnarled hooks gripping two large metal buckets filled with water. We were told he got the water at St Marie's cemetery. That was a long walk for something like water. I often wondered why he went so far when surely one of the neighbors would have given him water. He could have even gotten it at St. Marie's rectory. He never seemed to look up; he always seemed to be so sad. We often wondered if we should offer to help him but we never approached him; we were afraid.

I still remember the night in late summer. The oppressive heat of late August, the twinkling of the fireflies in the still evening air made it a lazy summer night. We were bored. Catching fireflies is only so exciting. We were hot, too hot to play one of our many games like kick the can or relievee-o. It was too dark to play football and too early to go home. Our bedrooms at home were at least ten degrees hotter than it was outside. We felt the need to do something different, something exciting. School was closing in on us and we felt edgy. Our firecracker and cherry bomb stockpiles were by now depleted. What to do? Who to do it to?

Go on a night raid for apples or cherries? Naw. Sure we sneaked into backyards, climbed the trees, got the best fruit and got out undetected. We knew that the people whose trees we were raiding knew we were raiding them and just let us get away with it. Oh, every once in a while, someone would come out and scare the bejesus out of us, but I guess they had boring nights, too. I forget whose idea it was but it really was greeted with gusto. Let's go scare the crap out of old Joe Goggles.

Our plan was to sneak up to the edge of the fence closest to his hut. We would then lob rocks onto his tin roof. If we did it right, it would be another Lenny Leed's firecracker adventure. Of course, scary noises, screams, howls, et cetera would follow the commotion that was being caused by rocks hitting metal over a hollow enclosure. Great fun, just what we needed. Another "what I did on my summer vacation" tale to be told not in front of the class, but outside at lunch or recess.

We headed down to the tracks to get rocks, which we stuffed in our pockets. Then it was up the tracks towards the path that took us to the Old Valley and the corner of old Joe's house.

God, I can still feel the sensation that started in the pit of my stomach, the cold shiver going up my spine. It was the anticipation of action, the uncertainty of the outcome, just like the starting kickoff of a football game or the feeling of starting up a ledge or down into a canyon, like the Grand Canyon. The feeling vanishes quickly as the action starts.

We giggled, pushed and shoved one another as we got closer to the unsuspecting victim. Good, he wasn't sitting outside, but his door was open. The faint glow from his kerosene lamp cast an orange reflection on the earth in front of the door. We could see his shadow pass by the doorframe.

We looked at one another, smiled and proceeded to throw our stones. The noise from the rocks when they hit the roof scared us so much that our screams were really frightened screams. The stillness of the night was shattered by what seemed to be even a more deafening sound than we anticipated. The look on the poor guy's face as he came screaming out of the hovel he called home just can't be described. At first, it seemed to be terror. That was quickly replaced by a look of bewilderment as he sensed he was in no real danger. However, the look that was etched into my mind that night was the look of sorrow that crossed his weather-beaten face, staring at us through those magnifying lenses of his glasses. His eyes were so wide they seemed to ask the question, "Why have you done this to me? Have

I ever . . . ?" He looked away from us, turned his head and sat heavily on his bench, his head buried in his hands, his shoulders heaving and shaking. He never looked back at us or said a word to us. I wish he had yelled, cursed or did something.

We ran, heads down, not looking at one another. Shame is too mild a word for what we felt. We had hurt a person who had never done any harm to us, or as far as we knew, to anyone else.

My bedroom that night was like an oven, like the hell I was headed for. How could I ever confess what I did? Every time I shut my eyes his face appeared. My sleep was fitful, my dreams unpleasant. When I woke, it was not yet dawn. The sheets of my bed were soaked with sweat. I felt mentally and physically exhausted. The next few days were not happy play days for us. Not the "eat, drink and be merry for school starts soon" days. My friends and I never spoke of that night. We were not bad kids, but we had done a bad thing. A lesson was taught us that night. A lesson none of us was anxious to repeat, for that night we saw the look of a defeated man.

Three days later my Pop told me to come out in the backyard with him. I felt uneasy, scared. Pop didn't usually do stuff like that. He looked me right in the eyes and said, "Guy, I don't want you to ever bother that man again. Do you hear me?" I nodded because I couldn't say a word. He turned and went back inside. I wonder how many other fathers told sons that message over the next few days. After that, we never walked by his hut if we could help it.

Thinking on this incident, I stand here on the corner looking at a shack that is only there in my mind. I wonder, why did old Joe have those blue numbers tattooed on his arm? Did his wife and children go toward the place he seemed to stare at so vacantly? What caused this man to shy away from people, even those who allowed him to live there undisturbed? Old Joe Goggles would disappear from our lives and our minds.

As we grew older, our interest in the valley was replaced by another kind of interest. A challenge we had to face and overcome was the age-old battle of the hormones. Our interest in other things blossomed as surely as the young ladies in our lives did. One day a few years later, I drove past old Joe's shack. It had been torn down. It startled me for a moment. I wonder, since I can't remember, if I thought maybe old Joe had finally stared himself to that place he seemed to want to be. Enough about old Joe.

⧗

Winter Street was one of the main avenues of our young lives. A good portion of my buddies lived on this street: my best friends Jim, Sean, the Breslin brothers and Rich Mulligan, who was the only kid I knew at the time that had no brothers or sisters.

Mr. Timlyn lived on Winter Street. Mr. Timlyn was an old man. He was a retired blacksmith. He had plied his trade at different mines repairing broken tools and equipment. Mr. Timlyn was a big burly man whose hands reminded me of big baseball mitts. His rough exterior hid a man with a gentle heart and a flair for growing apples and other tasty fruits. His backyard was like a disorganized orchard. "Here a tree, there a tree, everywhere a tree, tree." On one of his trees grew the biggest, juiciest apples I have ever eaten. I swear they were twice the size of a normal apple. When we bit into one, the juice squirted out and dripped down our little dirt-coated hands. Mr. Timlyn never chased us away when we raided his fruit trees.

Mr. Timlyn had a dog to befit both his size and disposition. He had a St. Bernard that was as big as a Shetland pony. My pop would occasionally visit Mr. Timlyn in the evenings. They sat on the porch and exchanged stories, tales and relived times they worked together at various mines. Pop brought me along. I don't remember these excursions clearly but I can piece together fragments here and there. Mr. Timlyn and Pop used to put me on the dog's back like he was a horse. The dog would walk patiently around the yard with his wannabe Lone Ranger on his back. There are pictures somewhere taken by someone that prove this story. From what I was told the dog and I became fast friends. He was tolerant of my pestering young nature, allowing me to tug on his ears or whatever. Patience has its limits.

One very hot summer night I was more than a little annoying to the gentle giant of a dog. My pop laughed when he told my mom how the dog, tired and hot, just lifted his huge paw, placed it on my shoulder and pinned me beneath him. Struggle as I might I couldn't free myself so I just lay there. When I relaxed enough, the dog let me up. I then proceeded to prop my back against this rather warm patient animal and fell fast asleep. This would have made a great picture but unfortunately no one had a camera.

⧗

I can see the change in the houses. They are remodeled structures, some with their beloved porches gone. Most have been modernized. Sears siding on some. Brick facing on others. Most have bigger windows, newer roofs. I guess they were changed as new, younger residents molded these homes to fit their lives.

Rich and Jim's houses sat on one side, Tucker's and Sean's on the side where St. Marie's Grade School is. The grade school still looms like a huge brick castle for it was built to last. It has not changed. The three-storied structure seems as impressive as it did when I was a kid.

I don't have to enter the school to know its interior. It probably has not changed at all. I put in eight-plus years of my young life roaming those hallowed halls of learning. On the first floor is an auditorium, complete with stage. The well-worn wooden floor hosted both adult and children's dances. Every year the local men and women got together and put on a minstrel show before a packed house. The townspeople sat through matinees and evening perfor-mances on no-nonsense wooden chairs. During these shows local comedians poked fun at friends and neighbors. Children did their best imitations of Van Cliburn. Housewives sang, boys and girls tap-danced and the men got up and made fools of themselves all to benefit St. Marie's Church, School and Convent.

Smokers were held there. Men gathered and watched famous films of Notre Dame football games. Local sports legends and famous men like Mr. Crawley, one of the four horsemen of Notre Dame, came and spoke.

Children gathered here for singing lessons. We sang praises to our Lord and His mother. We heralded the saints and angels. We sang Latin songs of the old church Mass. We harmonized with such great show tunes as "I Am the Captain of the Pinafore" and "My Grandfather Clock." Girls with their angelic voices carried over the boys' rough tones. The boys' voices always managed to emphasize "the balls whistling free o'er the bright blue sea," or to rhyme "my grand clock" and "jock" to give new meaning to an old song.

The auditorium served as a reception hall for weddings, a meeting place for parents and by far the most important function, bingo. Bingo was the financial backbone of both church and school.

Pop called the numbers. My brothers and sisters, my friends and I checked the winning cards. The room was filled to capacity. Pop called B-10 or I-19. The loud, joyous cry, "Bingo!" would be followed by Pop's loud, booming voice warning, "Do not clear the cards until the numbers are checked."

I remember both playing and checking cards. The excitement mounted with each game. Winner after winner, their cards checked and cleared, moved us toward that final big money pot. The final game had multiple winners. The first part was four corners, then diagonal, then straight across or up and down, round robin, then to fill the card. One person usually won and that left a few hundred disappointed folks who couldn't wait until next month's game. The only interruption of the bingo schedule in our parish was Lent.

Lent caused the pursuit of all earthly pleasures to stop. Lent was taken very seriously. For the next forty days smokers kicked the habit. Others gave up drinking, and for those men that would surely earn them a place near the Almighty in heaven. People started diets. Radios and TVs fell silent. Families prayed the rosary. People attend early daily Mass. I guess that's why we didn't really mind kneeling for three straight hours on Good Friday. We could see light at the end of the tunnel. The sale of cigarettes, cigars, pipe and chewing tobacco soared on Good Friday. Cases of beer were iced. There would be no more hot cross buns and no more fish on Wednesday as well as Friday. TV, radio and movies were once more allowed as entertainment.

As kids we entered the school building through the front or back doors and headed to the second and third floors. This was the functional area. The second floor was reserved for grades one through four, with the first grade all the way to the back of the hall on the right, second grade on the left, third grade on the right and fourth opposite third. Also on the second floor was a room we avoided at all cost: Mother Superior's office. Personally, I would rather have lost an arm or leg than be summoned there. Believe me it was one long, lonely walk. A nun did not become Mother Superior by accident. I often wondered if they attended the same training course as marine drill instructors. I've had experience with both and if given the choice, I'd rather have a DI chew me out, for Mother Superior's wrath knew no end.

My experience at St. Marie's started much earlier than first grade. My sister, Anne, used me for show and tell. Father Nilus, my uncle, was a career army chaplain. When he returned from Europe, he brought a miniature pair of wooden shoes from Holland. My sister Anne noticed that these shoes fit my tiny feet, so periodically I was taken to school where these wooden blocks were placed on me. Then I marched around the room clippity-clopping all the way.

Anne taught me little songs, then brought me to school to sing them. I remember standing in front of her class doing my renditions of "Rubber Ducky, I Love You" and the one Anne and her classmates relished the most, "I'm a Little Teapot" complete with hand and body movements. I was too young to be embarrassed; besides everyone always said how cute I was doing these little routines. I'm so glad they never put me in any of the minstrel shows. I never would have lived it down.

Another cute little thing that got me attention was pronouncing my L's like W's. Older kids and adults were always asking me to say things like "little world," "long day" or "last week." When I said them, they came out "wittle world," "wong day," and "wast week." A neat little Elmer Fudd imitation and it always got laughs.

My first grade teacher was a patient, kind person. Kids liked her; she liked kids. She was a pleasant young nun. She was unable to change my "wittle" speech impediment. My second grade teacher was Mother Superior of the convent and principal of the school. She was neither young nor pleasant. I will always remember my first day in second grade. Mother Frances asked me a question. My answer unfortunately contained a few L's and W's. She was not amused. "Jeri, step out into the hall, please." "Yes, Mother." Poor naïve Jeri was to learn a lesson. "Now, Jeri, I want you to say little world," she emphasized little. "Yes, Mother, wittle world." I never saw the slap coming; she really had fast hands. "Now, Jeri, I want you to say little world."

I was still in shock. My reply was reflexive and gargled: "wittle world." Whack. I didn't see that one either. Boy, was she fast. "Say it right, Jeri." I paused and thought carefully. The articulated words came out low but clear: "little world." I shut my eyes as I uttered those two little words. "I knew you could do it, young man. Now go in there and take your seat." I sobbed, "Yes, Mother." My speech therapy had been short and to the point. I never again pronounced my L's like W's.

My oldest brother, Francis, was in high school by the time I started St. Marie's. My sister, Anne, and brother, Don, were still there when I started. Anne, like a lot of older sisters, was assigned the task of taking care of me when Mom was not on duty. Anne led me to school in the morning and walked home with me at lunch. In the morning, she wet and combed my hair into fancy waves. This was fine with me. I didn't have to do it myself. The only time I really didn't like this was in the winter. Winters in the area are cold and snowy, but I was kind of lucky since we lived very close to school. On these cold mornings, Anne and me walked hand in hand to school, not a long walk for her but my little legs only went so fast. Every morning upon arrival at school my hair was frozen. Anne never noticed and I never said anything because I thought it was neat.

Going to school in winter required proper clothing. The mothers' choice to keep their precious young charges warm was the snowsuit, complete with mittens. These mittens were never lost. They were secured to the suit by string so strong it could tow a car. Vesting and unvesting was a Herculean task. One winter afternoon I was walking back to school after lunch, my snowsuit slowing my pace. I passed a puddle caused by melting ice and snow. Now what kid could resist splashing other unsuspecting kids by jumping feet first into the puddle? This was my chance and I wasn't going to waste it. I jumped, hit the ice and slid into the water. I was in trouble. My body lay prone in the water; I was flapping like a beached fish; I couldn't get up. Water saturated my suit. I now weighed twice my body weight. Kids were laughing but not helping me out. Jim saw my dilemma and came to my rescue. He and a kid he coerced into helping pulled me out. I was freezing. What to do?

Mom would not be happy. Sister Myra would not be happy. And I was not happy. Now I knew my happiness would not be a major concern to either Mom or the good Sister. I had a tough choice to make: go home and face Mom or go to school and face Sister Myra. Jim inadvertently made the decision for me by saying, "Geez, Jeri, your mom is going to kill you." Right, off to school I went. I left a long trail of ice water all the way to my third grade class. To say I was embarrassed would be an understatement. A good prank had gone bad. I'd be as old as Methuselah, whoever he was, before the other kids let me live this one down.

Sister Myra heard me squishing my way into the room. "Young man, what did you do? Well, I'm waiting."

Yeah, she was waiting, hand on what I believed to be her hip. It was hard to tell. Nuns wore habits. I know snowsuits had a lot of material in them but it was nowhere near the forty or fifty yards of heavy blue cloth that covered every part of a nun's body except for her hands. Their hands, lethal weapons that they were, had to be free for action at any given moment. A huge, tight black belt surrounded the middle. In the belt they kept items crucial to their lives. A beautiful long rosary hung from the side. When they turned suddenly, the rosary looped out and formed a swathing path about eighteen inches from the body. We tried hard not to startle them or we would receive an unintended lash. Hidden somewhere in the belt was the sturdy wooden ruler. Believe me that ruler was used for more than drawing straight lines. They wore a huge hard snow-white breastplate that hung from a starched Roman collar surrounding their neck. A black veil-covering, a crescent-shaped, white headdress and a starched white forehead cover completed their uniform.

I was standing there dripping, an ever-increasing puddle of water surrounding me. I had to look up to her. Nuns, like mothers, need eye contact at all times. "Look at me, and don't forget that I can tell if you are lying." That phrase was burned in my brain at a very young age. "Well young man, I'm waiting."

If I hadn't been so cold I would have been sweating.

"Don't you have anything to say for yourself?" A thought flashed through my mind. Yeah, I fell in a wittle puddle of water on my way down the wane. Jeri, this isn't funny. "Maybe you'd like to explain to Mother Frances how you got so wet." That did it. "Yes Sister, I slipped and fell in a puddle." "Well, young man, why didn't you say so? Go over there and sit on that radiator until you dry out." "Yes, Sister."

That started what was to be a two hour and forty minute preview of hell. Oh, at first I felt good. Cold turned to warmth, warmth turned to heat, heat turned to steam. I was being parboiled. "Sit still over there, Mr. Docerty." Sit still! My butt was on fire. I tried everything I could imagine to ease my discomfort. I offered it up for the poor souls in purgatory, but after a half hour, I figured, "Let them burn, I am. I am burning." Then I tried imagining snow falling on my outstretched naked body, but all that came to mind was the annual Labor Day Clam Bake in Finagin's backyard. I don't know how I got through that afternoon but I did. By the time the last prayer was said and school was dismissed I was only slightly damp. I took the back steps two at a time, out the back door of the school into the cool January afternoon air. I had made it. I escaped purgatory, I was in heaven and it was cool. I can still feel the steam after all these years.

The schoolyard has been paved, but the black pipe fence that surrounded the perimeter of the convent yard survived. It's wider by about two inches; painting probably expanded its girth. I used to feel sorry for Sean and Jim, but particularly Sean. His house and yard bordered the whole school on the right. I'd get chills playing in his yard over the summer. A sudden glance up would trigger a psychic episode, a classroom window, math and spelling. Geez!

"Let's go over to Jim's." I don't think Sean cared for his situation any more than I did.

I can't remember how I felt about starting first grade. My brothers and sister went so I guess I just accepted it with no real fear. I didn't have to be dragged screaming out the front door. Not going to school certainly could be boring and somewhat dangerous in my case.

⧖

Mom always believed that a child belonged outside playing, so every day Mom put me outside. Every day Bart Barre, who was about my age, trudged across the street to play with me. Our ideas of play were at opposite ends of the spectrum. My idea involved running and games. His idea involved punching me repeatedly about the body and face. Bart was clever, Mom never saw him or his style of play and I was too dumb to tell her. One day my oldest brother Fran was home sick. He was really sick. One thing kids in my neighborhood never did was miss school. Mom cooked, cleaned and generally worked hard, sick or not. Pop and the other fathers went to work every day; sick or hurt, they never missed. Their kids would do no less.

On this particular day, Bart was whaling me about the body as usual. Unbeknownst to me, my brother watched in disbelief from the window. I was allowed in after a fair amount of color had been brought into my cheeks by the cold. He called me into the living room and asked why I didn't punch him back. "I don't know." He then proceeded to give me my first boxing lesson. I caught on quickly.

The next day I waited, a slight smirk on my face. I was ready. Bart came into the yard. I held back waiting. Ten minutes went by, nothing. The he started. First the little shove. I went with it as usual. Then I saw his arm draw back. Go ahead, Bart.

He punched. I blocked and counterpunched. Right jab to the head. It was all over. Blood trickled out of Bart's nose. He looked stunned. All of a sudden he broke into tears, put his head down and ran crying from the yard. All right, Jeri.

When Mom called me in for lunch I was really proud. I couldn't wait to show my brother Fran how Bart ran away in tears. I wolfed down my bowl of tomato soup and my bologna sandwich, left the table and went into the living room to practice Bart's flight from the yard in defeat. I did it at least three times. I wanted it to be perfect. After all, it was my big brother that I wanted to impress. The fourth time, my head lowered, my arms moving like pistons, I ran full force into the radiator. This split my skull, or should I say my scalp, since I've been told my skull was too thick to hurt. My brother arrived home from school. He looked at me sitting on the couch, my head wrapped in gauze. I stared vacantly into space.

"Hey, what happened, Jeri?"

I couldn't speak, my head hurt too much. I tried to form words to share the epic tale with my brother but the only words that were heard were those of my mother. "I don't know what's the matter with that boy; he ran headfirst into the radiator."

My brother looked at me and just shook his head. He didn't say it but I knew he was thinking, "Geez, that kid is dumb."

By the time my turn came to enter school, the family reputation had been established. My older brother Francis, always a hard worker, achieved much. My sister Anne was smart, pretty and also a hard worker. She was loved and respected by all. Then there was my brother Don. Well, Don's another story. He's probably the most intelligent in the family. He was a hard worker, but not in school. He was also a hell-raiser. He drove Mom and Pop nuts, but he had a good heart and when it came to excelling, he did, but only when he wanted to. It was almost as if he'd lead the nuns to a certain point and then he'd kick in his afterburner and win an academic award. This really ticked Sister Bertha off. I think that's why he did it, just to piss her off.

So my turn came and much was expected of me. Aw, there were such great expectations. The apple doesn't fall far from the tree, et cetera. Well, when I hit the ground I must have rolled down the hill because I wasn't even in the orchard. I tried and tried but complicated material like "See Spot. See Spot run. Run, Spot, run," just floored me. Besides everyone knows dogs run, why do I have to read about it?

"Jeri, spell cat." "K-A-T." "No, what sounds like a K?" "Geez, I don't know."

Another thing about spelling was where to put an I. I before E, except after C. Oh yeah, right. Then they asked me to spell neighbor, which of course I spelled nieghbor.

"No, Jeri that's not right." Hold it, Sister. Will ya make up your mind.

It never got any easier. Neighbor gave way to weigh followed by reign. Other things like right, write, or turn right. Then the reign of terror took place in an awful rainstorm while the peasants tried to seize the reins of power.

Learning at St. Marie's was a matter of repetition. We recited facts over and over until they were firmly embedded in our minds. Every subject was pounded into us every day, day in, day out. As I sit here perched on the black metal pipe staring up at the fortress of learning that is St. Marie's, I'm thankful for those lessons and the discipline that teaches self-discipline and thus leads to real learning. The nuns never let up on us. I admire their dedication. They lived a very austere existence devoid of many of the pleasures we take for granted. They lived their lives for what they believed in. I've heard people who were products of the nun's discipline complain, "They did this or they did that." Many of these same people lead successful productive lives as a result of the education given them by these women.

⧖

The eight years of formal education seemed to pass as quickly as our summer vacations. As the years passed, more and more responsibility was placed on our young shoulders. Safety patrol boys, sacristy aides, altar boys, as the grade levels increased so did our prestige. One of the more spectacular of school events was watching the school population move from school to church, either for Mass practice or some other religious event.

149

In school, the hand-held bell was rung. Its steady, rhythmic sound echoed down the hallowed halls of learning. From first to eighth grades we rose as one, lined up by height and sex and waited until word came to move out. Then the eighth grade led the top four grades to the edge of the third story landing and paused for a few moments. Repeated warnings of "Silence, young man," or "Stop that giggling, young lady" were taken to heart. Our eyes fixed on the person's head in front of us as we moved with the precision of an elite combat unit. The noise of feet on steps rose as more and more students descended the three flights of stairs to the front door. The first two boys in line each took a door, opened it and stayed their post until the tiniest of the first graders passed. These young men then secured the doors and fell in behind their miniature charges. As the column moved towards the church, four young patrol boys jogged ahead and acted as road guards. Two went ahead to Winter Street and the other two took positions on Blackthorne Street. The column hesitated three times before entering the church. Once at Blackthorne Street, then a momentary pause at Winter Street and finally at the bottom of the church steps. At the steps two more eighth grade boys quickly made their way to the church doors and opened them. Then the eighth grade entered, boys on the right, girls on the left. The eighth grade moved to the front of the church and stopped. A loud click echoed through the church. It triggered a mass genuflection. Another click, a mass rising, a third click sent students filing into pews. Class after class repeated this same procedure until finally all eight grades were in place. Mother Frances then walked up the main aisle and turned, then two more loud clicks and we all knelt, perfectly straight. The clickers must have been standard issue for the nuns. They all had them, but we never saw them for they were secreted somewhere on the good sister's person.

⧗

The school is directly opposite my buddy Jim's house. It kind of looks the same. Probably has a more modern basement than the old dirt one. I wonder if we were left alone long enough, whether we could have tunneled across Winter Street to the school. It seemed like a real fine idea at the time.

How many times did I stand outside that small kitchen porch at the side of the house and raise the call, "Hello, Jim. Hello, Jim." That was a standard procedure for calling on friends in the neighborhood.

Mrs. McAndrews would usually yell, "Come on in, Jeri, he's upstairs getting dressed." "Morning, Mrs. McAndrews, how are you today?" "Fine, Jeri, would you like a glass of Kool-Aid and some cookies?" "Yes, please."

What a bunch of moochers we were. By the time we all gathered on a summer morning, we were stuffed with cookies and Kool-Aid. Moms always kept plenty of grape-flavored, super sweet Kool-Aid. They also maintained an assortment of homemade cookies or the old standby, graham crackers. I loved graham crackers.

We never entered a house uninvited; that was a big no-no, but we were never turned away. Even if Jim wasn't home, Mrs. McAndrews, or whatever other mom it happened to be, would invite me in. If Jim weren't home, it meant he was somewhere having fun, so I'd politely refuse and head to another house or play area. There was no use wasting valuable playtime.

I don't know why, but we all called for each other at the back porch. All the houses in the area had a back porch and the porch led into the kitchen. The kitchen seemed to be the heart of the house. Families gathered at the kitchen table to eat and socialize. When friends came over to visit, they usually ended up in the kitchen for tea, milk, soda or Kool-Aid. While they were home on leave, my brothers would sit at the table and tell us about their air force adventures. My sisters and their friends met here to bake cookies or make chocolate fudge. My cousins Maureen and Cathy sat with me and shared secrets. Even today when I visit my brothers or sisters, we seem to always end up in the kitchen sharing our life stories.

I'm tempted to walk across the street, to recapture the past, to call once again, "Hello, Jim. Hello, Jim." I'd love to be able to run back through time the same way we ran through Jim's backyard. It was a shortcut to the alley and fields beyond. It led us to Joe Grady's house, the Old Field, New Field and to all the places where we played.

Jim's house triggers other memories. Memories I buried many years ago. Jim's was the same house where I spent the night of my father's death. Our house was a rush with friends and relatives. They were preparing for the arrival of my father's body. Like all families in the area, my family would wake my father's body in the family home. Mrs. McAndrews took me home with her around 7:30 that evening. She sat me down at their kitchen table and fixed me something to eat. Jim sat with me. Mrs. McAndrews left us alone. I picked at the food; it had no taste. Jim looked at me but looked away each time I looked up. Mrs.

McAndrews came back into the kitchen, "Jeri, you really should try to eat something; you'll need your strength." Normally, I would have been waiting for a second helping but that night I couldn't swallow; the food stuck in my throat. Jim got up, put his hand on my shoulder and said, "Let's go for a walk." I nodded, realizing that those were the first real words I had heard him speak that day. We walked out into that cold December night, down Winter Street, toward Kraft's Mill. We walked slowly as Jim measured his steps with mine. My legs felt like rubber, my brain was numb, my chest as hollow as an empty barrel. My breath shone like a white mist. I gasped as I fought so hard to stop the tears. Men don't cry.

Men don't cry. That thought made the struggle for control even more difficult. God, I hurt so bad. I tried praying but nothing happened. I felt Jim's arm around my shoulder even though it really wasn't. We just walked side by side down a cold dark street. The cold air brought strength back into my legs. My head cleared but my chest still remained empty. I can still hear the sound of our footsteps in the still night air.

I can't remember how long we walked but eventually we passed Kraft's Mill, took the path to the tracks and walked back toward Polack Hill. We turned up the path to Blackthorne Street and as we neared the church Jim said, "Do you want to stop in?" "No," was all I could make myself say. I didn't want to stop. What I really wanted was to wake from this horrible nightmare.

We entered Jim's house through the front door. His sisters and parents were watching a Frankenstein movie in the living room. We sat on the floor in front of the TV. I stared at the screen but saw nothing. When the movie ended, Mrs. McAndrews said, "Jeri, you can sleep in Jim's room. There's clean sheets and a pillow there for you."

"Thank you, Mrs. McAndrews."

She walked over to me and gave me the biggest, warmest hug. Her face touched mine and I could feel the warm, wetness of tears flowing down my cheek. At first I thought I had finally broken down and cried. Then I realized they weren't my tears.

Jim and I went to his room. Jim said, "Jeri, you sleep on the bottom bunk." I knew that was where he always slept; he didn't like the top bunk.

"Thanks, Jim." I lay there hoping to sleep and just maybe when I woke, this bad dream would finally end.

Jim's voice startled me, "You know my pop can't go to the corpse house. He can't see your father, I heard him telling my mom. He can't see your dad. He hasn't sounded that bad since my uncle got killed."

"I know Jim. I wish I didn't have to see him that way either." I finally fell asleep. I don't remember dreaming, just waking up in Jim's bunk knowing that it all wasn't a dream.

Jim and I talked about his father a week later. He explained something about how his father felt about death. I understood and felt deeply for this man. He had seen his share of death and just couldn't face the loss of another friend.

My turn to drive a car finally came. When I got my permit, Mr. McAndrews offered to teach me to drive. Anne had given me a few lessons, but Mr. McAndrews said it would be better if a non-family member taught me. When my permit came, he patiently took me under his wing and taught me the finer points of driving. He took me down on a Saturday for my driver's test, which I failed. He reassured me that the State had never passed a boy on his first test.

He said he'd work on my parallel parking the following day after Mass. The next day he took me out for my final driving lesson. I parked and parked until I was blue in the face. Finally he said, "You're ready, Jeri."

"Thanks for teaching me, Mr. McAndrews." I reached for the door handle to get out of the car. He reached over and gently touched me on the arm and said, "Jeri, I just couldn't face seeing your pop dead; that's why I wasn't at the corpse house." When this burly man looked at me, he looked so sad. He had lost a friend and had trouble dealing with that tragedy. He had lost too many friends, too many times before. I looked at him and said, "I know. Jim told me."

⧗

I'd better get moving, it's getting late and I have to get to the cemetery before dark. The walk back down Blackthorne Street to the now paved alley is a short one. Turning left takes me back towards the same path Jim and I took to reach the tracks that December night so many years ago. Like many other things in town, the alley has caught up with the times. Now it is not the dirt and rocks that every year was spread lightly with oil to keep the dust down. It was now paved. We played countless numbers of games of touch and tackle football in this alley. We played hide the flag, kick the can, relievee-o and red rover, red rover. It was during a game of red rover that I got the wind knocked out of me for the first time in my life. It happened late one evening as the light faded. It would soon be 9:00 P.M. and town curfew would sound. This whistle marked the end of the day's play for us.

155

"Red rover, red rover, let Mary come over." Mary hit the opposing line but failed to break through. Darn, we were losing. It was their turn. "Red rover, red rover, let Richie come over." Richie broke through.

We needed someone to break through their line. "Red rover, red rover, let Jeri come over." I headed at full speed toward Eddie Maroski. I figured that was their weakest point. When I hit, Eddie just let go and stuck out his foot. I tripped and flew into the air. When I hit the ground, I landed on a brick. The brick made solid contact with my solar plexus. I rolled around on the ground, gasping for air, but no air entered my lungs. Oh God, I'm dying and I can't even say an act of contrition. Another thought surfaced. I'll kill him. What a dirty guy. I knew we shouldn't let him play with us, that sneak. It was too late now. I thought I was dying, my friends thought I was dying and the would-be killer, Eddie Maroski, thought I was dying so Eddie took off for home.

I never knew I could hold my breath so long. It would have been a spectacular feat if I were doing it on purpose, but I wasn't. Precious air finally made its way slowly back into my lungs. Now the only thing I was left with was a beautiful red rectangle imprinted on my chest. The next day that pretty red mark became a black and blue mass of ugliness. It was a good gross out which I flashed in front of the girls in the neighborhood. I just lifted my T-shirt and they'd say, "Oh, that's disgusting." If it hadn't hurt so much I would have loved having it, but it did hurt. Whatever feeling my friends and I had for Eddie Maroski ended that night. My buddies and I swore vengeance. We'd get him, sooner or later.

Our chance for revenge came later that summer. An old Polish woman, Mrs. Jeddick, owned one of the few houses located on that alley. She lived there with her son and daughter. We bedeviled that poor family, but we did so unintentionally. It all started with Tucker Breslin and a kid named Pat from West Pleasant Dale. On Halloween night the year before, Tucker and Pat sneaked into the Jeddick's backyard and tipped their outhouse over. What they didn't know was that the old lady was sitting in it at the time. It not only scared the hell out of the old lady, it scared the hell out of Tucker and Pat.

Ever since that night her daughter made our young lives miserable. If one of our baseballs entered their yard, she took it. She amassed quite a few of our items over the course of that year. We thought about raiding her garage to get them back, but she watched her yard like a hawk. Finally, we decided on a course of action that almost had disastrous results. Their house bordered on two fields. The field between Grady's house and their house we called the Old Field. It was our favorite hangout. The field on the other side of their house was called the New Field. In that field grew tall grass that dried in late summer to a blondish color. This field was extremely susceptible to fire.

Our plan was to set a matchbook and cigarette time bomb in the field. First we would light the cigarette, place it behind the matches, then toss it casually into the field. Next, we would make ourselves very visible playing a game of touch football in front of their house. About five minutes later a fire broke out in the field. I never saw anything burn so fast. Holy shit, we had done it now.

Our aim was to quickly put the fire out and play the role of heroes. The daughter would be so grateful she'd give all of our baseballs back to us.

Miss Jeddick and her mother spotted the fire and ran out of the house. We were in the field trying to stomp out the fire, but it was getting bigger. Miss Jeddick ran back into the house and when she came out she was carrying about four rugs. "Here, use these boys." They had no phone. She yelled for one of us to run and get the firemen. Spike took off running. He got about as far as Mr. Timlyn's front porch. "Hold on there, Spike. What's your hurry?" "Mrs. Jeddick's field is on fire." Mr. Timlyn hurried inside to phone the hosey. By the time the firemen got there, we really had a blaze on our hands. We fought the flames valiantly, but until the firemen arrived it was a lost cause. Once again we lucked out. We weren't the only lucky ones. If it weren't for the firemen, Mrs. Jeddick's house would have been history.

Miss Jeddick and her mother were so grateful for our help they returned all of our confiscated property. They praised us as heroes. The firemen were impressed. "You boys did a great job." Then one of the firemen said, "I wonder how it started." Uh-oh, this could be trouble. Then the proverbial light bulb flashed on. "I saw Eddie Maroski running up the tracks." I looked over at Jim. "Yeah, yeah," Jim said, "I saw him, too." One by one each of us related our eyewitness accounts. We had seen Eddie coming out of the field and then running up the tracks toward his house. Spike finally said, "I bet he did it." His statement was reinforced by a series of "Yeahs." Eddie was the arsonist. Ah, vengeance is sweet.

The only truth to that entire story was that we had seen Eddie walking on the railroad tracks. We had framed an innocent lad. No one saw much of Eddie over the next few months. Oh, we saw him at school but he was not happy to see us. Eddie was not very successful in convincing his father that he hadn't been down in that field smoking a cigarette or that the cigarette had not caused a fire that could have burned down a house. Back then we did not use the word "grounded." We just were not allowed to do anything; that was our punishment. In Eddie's case, he would not have been "grounded," he would have been buried. Eddie would have had better treatment in Alcatraz.

The New Field belonged to the Jeddicks, so it was kind of off limits to us. The Old Field was the really important place. It was more of a huge vacant lot than a field. I don't know who owned it. No one ever stopped us from playing there. Kids from the neighborhood always used the place. About a quarter of the field was covered with bushes. The bushes covered the whole lower left-hand side of the field. Within those bushes was a maze of manmade, or I should say child-made, tunnels. Over the years, kids had made it into a great hiding place. We crawled in these bushes starting in the spring when they came into bloom. Those tunnels shielded us from prying eyes. We played for hours. One minute we were spies, the next, soldiers in the jungle.

The rest of the field was a jumble of old "foxholes" or "bunkers." They were dug out, filled in and dug out again. Each succession of kids built on or tore down the previous group's work. Many hours were spent on construction projects. Dig this hole deeper, reinforce this wall, find materials to build a roof or branches to act as camouflage. Some of our "bunks" turned out really nice. We built secret entrances and lit the interiors with lanterns made from candles. The insides of the holes were padded with old rugs or a mattress, if we could find one. In these "bunks" we held secret meetings to plan games and choose sides. In summer, it was a cool area protected from the rays of the sun. In winter it kept us out of the snow and cold wind.

We played a lot of war games in the Old Field and to make the games more realistic, we constructed traps and planted our equivalent of landmines. Our landmines consisted of digging a shallow hole and placing a small balloon in the bottom of it, then covering the balloon with dirt and grass. They were really neat; when you stepped on them they popped and blew a little dust and grass up in the air. We planted so many of these we lost track of where they were, so it was not uncommon to suffer a sprained ankle running through the field.

One of the best things about the Old Field was the weenie roasts we had there. Like the kids before us we'd use an old firepit. We would build up the rocks around it and then go to collect firewood. We all built fairly good fires since we used coal to heat our houses. We had been taught the proper way to start a coal fire so building a wood fire was easy. We held a lot of these roasts starting in early May and ending around Halloween. Every couple of weeks we would get the urge. Nobody had to be invited. Everyone was welcome, in fact, the more the merrier. Our bill of fare was simple. Hot dogs and rolls, unless it was held on a Friday. We could always count on someone bringing a large jar of French's yellow mustard. Potatoes were a must; everyone brought at least two. We placed the potatoes in a circle around the inside of the firepit where they roasted as the fire burned. Soda was also another staple; everyone usually brought a couple of bottles. Then there were the marshmallows. To cook our hot dogs and marshmallows, we each selected a choice branch from a small tree. It was green wood so it wouldn't catch fire easily. The best sticks had small forks in them. We sharpened these into prongs with a penknife. I really enjoyed sitting around the fire roasting hot dogs, laughing, telling stories and eating.

When all the hot dogs were gone, we'd stab into the potatoes in the firepit and see which ones were done. Eating charred, blackened potatoes cooked in the firepit provided some of the best potatoes I've ever eaten. The skin crunched as we bit into these tasty spuds. Once the skin of the potato was broken its steaming white contents were spread with margarine and sprinkled with salt. By the time we'd finish our potatoes, our faces had acquired a blackened oval around our mouths. We looked as if we had been eating charcoal and enjoying it. With the hot dogs and potatoes eaten, our teeth and faces flaked with bits of potato skin and our bellies distended with food, we'd lay back on the warm, grass-covered earth and stare up with wonder at the star-brightened sky. Our conversation was subdued as we sipped warm soda and belched contentedly waiting for our stomachs to digest our roasted evening feast. We all relaxed in the quiet stillness. The darkness of the night began to conjure up in our minds legendary stories of horror.

There were tales of UFOs, devils and demons, monsters and ghostly tales of dead prom queens appearing on lonely country roads. Our imaginations pictured escaping mass murderers who axed or hooked their unsuspecting victims in the most gruesome of fashions. Our minds were working at a feverish pitch, each hoping to be able to tell the story that would scare our friends to death.

As time passed and our bodies slowly absorbed the food, we would become restless and hungry again. This time we needed something sweet, something white, sugary and hot, so the marshmallows were distributed evenly among us for we shared what we had. The white chunks were placed on the ends of our cooking sticks and stuck into the open flames. It didn't take long for them to catch fire signaling that they were ready for consumption. The secret to eating toasted marshmallows is to wait for a few seconds before putting them in your mouth, unless of course, you don't mind having hot gooey marshmallow stuck to the roof of your mouth.

When the marshmallows were all gone, the soda finished and more wood added to the fire, we proceeded with the entertainment for the evening. Jokes were told and retold, laughter echoed through the warm still night. Gossip was exchanged, but the real event, the one we eased into, was the ghost stories. What made these eerie tales so frightening was our close proximity to the coal flats. Our imaginations were always active but never so active as on these nights. All eyes and ears were riveted on the storyteller. I can still feel the thrill I felt as a kid. My mind and body would tense as these stories reached their inevitable bloody climactic ends. Some stories were so popular that they were told at almost every weenie roast.

⧗

So much of my childhood revolved around this immediate area. The memories have not faded. I can shut my eyes and see Jim, Joe, Sean, Tucker, Spike and all the rest of the guys and girls. We were all so young, so alive and oh so naïve.

Kids should grow up like this. We ran, jumped and played ourselves into strong, decent young men and women. We were free of so many of the things kids have to face today. We weren't fingerprinted and photographed just in case we were abducted by some pervert. We were taught to respect ourselves and others. We loved our mothers and fathers, our brothers and sisters. When one of our friends was hurting, we were all hurting. I wouldn't change this part of my life for all the money in the world.

My heart aches knowing that I have to leave, but I have to get back to the cemetery before dark. With my head down, I start walking towards the path near where old Joe Goggles used to live. The path will take me into West Pleasant Dale. My thoughts occupy me so much that time and distance blend. I pass some familiar places. There was the old Dean Phipps warehouse. I continue to walk down the hill past the Little League field. I'm walking faster than usual, but I'm not looking around much now. The only place I recognize as I walk down McAlpine Street toward the cemetery is my Aunt Catherine's old family home. Across the street from Aunt Catherine's old house is the house of some high school friends, Tom and Barbara Grace. I cover the three blocks to Cemetery Street rather quickly and as I cross that old metal bridge with the wooden planks, I can hear the funny hollow noises my feet make on the planking. It reminds me of the day Mom was buried.

As I sat in the limousine crossing the bridge that day, I could hear planks moan as they bore a weight heavier than that of a car. Time has dulled the pain but not the memory. Much of what happened growing up here in this small northeastern Pennsylvania town was filled with pleasant and happy times. It's really hard for me to fit these tragic events into that same period. I guess these bad times make the good times seem so much better.

I can see the van parked near the steps leading up towards the graves. Just a little farther and I will have come full circle. This journey has been more than just a walk around a small town; it has been a walk back through time, my time. The friends and family I shared this walk with are scattered, older or not even here anymore. It's been a day that has spanned the thirty years or more since I lived in what now seems to be that dreamtime.

I have no trouble finding the graves now. The small stone with its polished light gray luster seems to reflect the rays of a dying sun. As I look down at the name DONALD M. DOCERTY, I can also see etched invisibly below his name that of his beloved wife SADIE.

The air feels much as it did this morning. A light evening breeze makes its warmth feel pleasant. It won't be long before the cooler night air will turn the cemetery into a dark foreboding place. The ground will cool, the moisture will rise into the air and a tiny layer of dew will cover the graves like so many tears. I look up to the top of the hill and see an older woman tending a grave. She does so carefully, lovingly. A small pot of fresh flowers has been placed there. She seems bent over even though she is kneeling. If she stood, I would probably see her shoulders hunched over. It's a sad scene, for the grave looks fresh and she looks tired.

I look back to Mom and Pop's graves; they are old graves but the memories I have of them are not old. The words "if only" seem appropriate now. If only they could have seen me graduate from college. If only they had had a chance to see me coach a wrestling match or teach a class. If only they could have seen me perform in a karate demonstration. If only they could have played with their grandkids or been around to see my sister Mary Catherine get her doctorate degree or had been able to travel and visit with their sons and daughters to see firsthand their accomplishments.

I know deep in my heart they have seen these things. It's just that we never got to say thank you to them for giving us what it took to do these things. We didn't say we loved each other very often but love is so much more than words.

A friend of mine by the name of Peg once said to me, "Jeri, before you do that, think of what your mother would think of you." She was right because as I stand here I can feel both of them, Mom and Pop, inside me, pushing me, prodding me, urging me to try to live the way they taught me to.

Mom and Dad, I love you.